Bom
Over Brooklyn

By Brian J. Cline

Cover design by Brian J. Cline
and ummhumm | creative studio

CONTENTS

BRIAN J. CLINE

ACKNOWLEDGEMENT

Special shout out and proper thanks to my editor, J. Proctor.

BRIAN J. CLINE

PROLOGUE

A fresh bump of Bob Rock's premium blend rocketed its way up Tristan's nose and headed straight for his eagerly awaiting pleasure centers. Grinning, he wiped the remaining white residue off the cracked compact mirror with a fingertip before rubbing it deep into his gum line and settling in for an evening of post show mayhem.

Grant, the man of the hour sat at the head of the table with dancing eyes that gazed over the small crowd gathered around him. Suddenly, Tristan issued his usual heartfelt plea. "Again? You want to hear it again?" Grant replied.

When Tristan and the rest of the group gave a raucous response of agreement that hurt his ears, Grant laughed and ran the sure, confident fingers of a seasoned rock musician through his thick mane, again ready to narrate the epic tale that had now become the stuff of legend.

The scarred oak table at which they sat had borne witness to hundreds of after show parties; at this moment, it was packed with a new crop of rowdy, wide-eyed teen revelers all clad in leather, spikes, and lace. The group collectively piped down in anticipation of the fantastical account they knew was coming.

The consummate performer, Grant had every intention of giving the people what they wanted. He rolled his broad shoulders. Took a deep breath. Flashed his signature front man smile. Then, after a quick peck on the cheek from Dana, his platinum blonde moll, he began.

"So, it's early '82 and I'm working with this outfit selling bootleg concert t-shirts on the Ozzy Tour. We'd spent most of February crisscrossing the South, making money, getting high, and having a total blast. So right after the Knoxville show wrapped, we split and drove through the night straight to central Florida. *Blizzard of Oz* just went triple platinum and there was already talk of a bunch of

1

additional shows being added."

Grant paused for just a moment, and when not a single person blinked or moved a muscle, he knew he had them all in the palm of his hand.

"The sun was barely up when we pulled the truck off the turnpike into Orlando," he said as he continued, taking a quick sip of his beer. "We started getting everything unloaded early for the show, when out of nowhere, the sheriff's office rolled up on us with guns blazing. They wasted no time and proceeded to confiscate everything we had. Some of the crew managed to slip away, but they put me and another guy in cuffs and took us straight down to central booking. The company that was selling the legit tour merch must have tipped them off instead of having to deal with us themselves."

Grant had been beyond pissed at the time, so it took little effort to play up that expression on his face. He was pleased to see it reflected at him in the faces of his audience. Leaning forward, he braced his elbows on his knees to get more comfortable. He was getting to the good part.

"Okay, so I'm sitting there, handcuffed to a bench in this waiting room while they're processing my buddy. My adrenaline rush started tapering off and I realized just how fucked I was. I really started freaking out. I had a half ounce of weed stuffed in my crotch, three hundred in cash in my boot and a couple of priors on the books back up in New York. Listen, I'm a lucky son of a bitch, but I knew there was no way in hell I was getting out of this one. All of a sudden, I had a moment of clarity. I got this funny feeling that if I just pulled hard enough on the cuffs and started twisting my hands in all sorts of weird directions, they just might pop open. Ya' know...like Houdini or some shit. I looked around to make sure no one was watching me, asked St. Jude for a little technical assistance, and began."

The responding smattering of laughter grew louder when Grant made a show of pretending to get his hands loose from imaginary handcuffs. "About twenty or thirty seconds in, I'm pulling, twisting and grinding on these things like my life depended on it, 'cause it kinda did. All of a sudden – BAM!"

Grant reached up and slapped the table so hard, everyone jumped – even Tristan, and he'd lost count how many times he'd heard the story.

"The chain fucking snapped! Needless to say, I was in a state of shock. The chick behind the glass was out of sight and talking up a storm to one of the deputies about her kid's graduation or some shit, and I thought to myself 'it's now or never'. I rolled down my sleeves, got up slowly" – Grant did just that and stood in front of his chair – "then slipped out the back door like a ghost. It felt like something straight out of a movie, except in slow motion, like those dreams where someone's chasing you. It took me about twenty minutes and a half a bottle of hand soap in a truck stop bathroom to finally slide those shackles off. I still have the scars to prove it." Grant raised his hands and showed the captive audience the scar tissue bands snaking around both wrists.

"This is so fucking great!" Tristan said to no one in particular. In awe, he shook his head and kept watching.

Grant stopped to catch his breath, well aware that he had everyone at the table hanging on his every word. He cracked his knuckles and said "Hold on; it gets better. I found out the next bus back to New York was leaving from Leesburg at around nine-thirty. I hitched a quick ride from a bunch of hippies in a VW bus and made it to the bus depot right about nine. The birds were chirping away as I sipped my coffee outside the station. I was looking west and trying to wrap my head around what the hell had just happened, when all of a sudden, kaboom! There's an explosion. It sounded like a civil war cannon went off in the distance. Thick black smoke started billowing up through the trees and the sky started getting really hazy and weird."

If it were possible, everyone's wide eyes got wider.

3

"A little while later, the sound of fire engines and cop cars started coming from every direction. I had no idea what was going on. A few seconds later I heard the terminal dispatcher announce that the bus was going to start boarding. I had a hard time pulling myself away, but given the situation, I had to get a move on. So I went inside and validated my ticket, bought a newspaper and found an empty seat. I figured it was probably an eighteen-wheeler that wrecked or something. After that, I didn't even give it a second thought. Twenty-two painful hours later, I was home. I crawled through the front door looking and feeling like complete shit. I told Mom and Pops a half-baked version of what had really happened and went straight to bed." Grant's gaze fell to Tristan, who grinned as Grant continued. "The next morning, the phone rang. It was Tristan. He's like 'dude, I heard from your brother you were back in town – did you see the news last night?' And I'm like, 'no, why?' And he's all, 'Randy Rhodes died in a plane crash in Florida'."

The group gasped collectively, Tristan himself giving a sober nod. "How fucked up is that?" Grant said, throwing up his hands. "One of the greatest guitarists that ever lived, the guy they said gave Ozzy a second chance after Sabbath, dies in a fiery plane wreck and I was sitting there less than a football field away at the exact moment it happened. Crazy shit! I got very lucky that day. I only wish I could have thrown a little of it his way. Nobody deserves to go out like that, especially a living legend."

Tristan, now glassy-eyed and choked up, spit out an emphatic, "Un-fucking real! I remember you thought I was putting you on. It took a while for that one to sink in." He raised his beer up high, looked around the table and made a toast. "To Randy."

The group raised their beers in unison and shouted back: "To Randy!"

Grant, satisfied with his account of that day's events and the audience's positive response, slid back in his chair. He lit up a fresh cigarette and watched wistfully as the smoke rose up over the crowd. The cocaine and beer-fueled teen banter and earsplitting music continued to rage on into the wee hours.

CHAPTER 1

The rain soaking Brice Laine to the bone as he stepped off his shiny new extension ladder forced two questions into his mind: would the aluminum storm shutters he'd just blown a fortune on hold tight? And was his decision to move his family to south Florida a colossal error in judgment?

He didn't have an answer for either at the moment. That's what had his guts in a knot.

As Brice tried in vain to wipe the rivulets from his brow, the apocalyptic news images that had been bombarding him and the rest of the state's jittery residents on a nightly basis tumbled through his thoughts on repeat. The U.S. National Hurricane Center prediction models painted a grim picture. News anchors were already referring to the oncoming hurricane as "The Big One".

The tradition of naming these havoc-wreaking forces of nature started back in the 1950s and aside from the occasional "Igor" or "Sampson", most of the storms hid behind benevolent monikers like Ernesto or Katie. With sustained wind gusts of over 135 miles an hour, Hurricane Hilda was spinning like a top just west the Lesser Antilles. And it was looking like she might have an axe to grind with the southern half of the sunshine state.

Brice tripped over his own feet in his hurry back into the house to tie up the many loose ends on his already overloaded prep list. God, there was still so much to do...

"Hun, you're making a big puddle." Brice glanced up to see his wife, Vera, striding through the kitchen in a pair of cutoffs and a pink tank top gathering supplies as he stood just outside the doorway planning his next move. Things were too tense with the incoming storm for Brice to stop and appreciate the view the way he would on

7

a normal day. He barely had time to duck the dish rag she flung at his head to help remedy his current situation.

Smirking, Brice dried himself off enough to continue with the task at hand – a month's worth of bottled water and instant ramen that needed to be moved out of the hallway and up to the safety of storage shelves in the garage. He bent and grabbed the nearest twenty-four pack of plastic bottles. A sharp zing of blistering pain from his sciatic nerve told Brice he had roughly thirty minutes of strenuous activity left in him before two Percocets and an ice pack would enter the evening's equation.

His son and daughter – Caleb, age six, and Mara, age four – had been unusually quiet over the past hour or so but upon hearing Brice entering the living room, they decided it was time to kick up some dust. Sensing an oncoming ruckus, the family cat, Tabbie, high-tailed it out of the fray to the safety of the overstuffed laundry basket atop the dryer.

"What are you monkeys *doing*?" The last word Brice spoke came out as a groan when the pint-sized dynamos barreling toward him threw their little arms around his legs.

"We're just messing around, Daddy," Caleb said laughing, making his sister giggle into her hand.

Oh, to be a child without a care in the world. Brice smiled down at his babies. "Okay, well...don't push your luck. You know what a grouch Mommy can be when she gets mad." Brice finished in a stage whisper.

"I heard that!" came Vera's snappy voice from the kitchen, right on cue, making Brice and his kiddos laugh even harder.

As he got them settled down, the familiar sights and sounds of endless hurricane news updates on the TV began to taper off, the regularly scheduled programming once again resuming. Brice got the kids to sit still on the couch long enough for him to proceed to the garage at last.

A familiar melody from Brice's past stopped him dead in his tracks, the sudden movement jarring his back and making pain flare down the back of his left leg. The unmistakable baritone of Golden Age film star Joel Hammond proudly proclaiming *"They say they hear bombshells over Broadway"* hit him like a wrecking ball to the gut, triggering the same goose bumps it had when he'd first heard it two decades earlier as a street-wise teen with acne.

Swirling orchestral arrangements filled the room as Brice turned towards the television set with his mouth agape. It had been ages since he'd thought about those lyrics and sounds, let alone heard them aloud.

Bombshells over Broadway, the movie version of the 1950s musical told the tale of Private First Class Joe McGinty who falls in love with starlet Sable Knowles prior to shipping out to the South Pacific during World War Two. The show had run for a record eighteen hundred performances and surpassed all previous Broadway attendance records. Bristling with post-war optimism and a musical score that made even the most jaded theater critics toe-tapping believers, it quickly became a beloved institution to a generation of Americans who'd fought tyranny on two fronts and were now busy living their lives and making up for lost time.

It had always spoken to Brice on a deep level, even in his teens. He sat motionless as the movie's opening scenes played in Technicolor before his eyes just as they had years before real life and the responsibilities of adulthood came calling.

Mara climbed up onto his lap. "What's this, Daddy?"

"Yeah, what's this?" echoed Caleb. He scooted closer to Brice's side on the couch.

Brice gave Mara a squeeze and rubbed the back of Caleb's head. "Guys, this is something that brings back a lot of memories for me."

9

He watched Caleb wince at the show's grainy quality – a far cry from the high-definition format of anything Brice knew his son had seen on the kiddie channels he watched all the time with his sister.

Caleb shook his head in clear disapproval, dark hair falling into his eyes. "This looks really old!"

Brice had to grin at that. "That's because it is really old, buddy."

Mara stared up at Brice then, deep blue eyes a near-perfect match for her mother's. "Did you watch this with Grandma when you were little?"

"No, honey; I was a little older when I first saw this," Brice said.

"Why is everybody dressed so funny?" Caleb asked with such conviction, Brice laughed out loud.

"That was the style back then, kiddo."

Mara was back to giggling. "I like our clothes much better," she said, head already turned to scan the messy room for something to play with. They were losing interest in this outdated spectacle fast.

"Yeah, me too, sweetie. Okay, you guys" – Brice eased Mara off his lap and shooed Caleb off the couch – "go back to whatever mischief you were causing and make sure you both wash your hands before we have dinner," he said. "I'm not sure how many hot meals we're gonna get to enjoy before this storm hits."

Brice went back to watching the show as the kids ran off squealing and laughing again, memories from his tumultuous youth flooding in faster than the continual downpour outside.

****

Spring, 1987

The opening power chords to the Seducer's Charm anthem "We Own the Night" played loudly in his head as seventeen-year-old Brice chewed his lip and fidgeted while waiting for the traffic light to change.

While unusually muggy March weather made Brice's t-shirt stick uncomfortably to his chest and back, it also had all the slender Upper East Side women wearing next to nothing – to the delight of the neighborhood bike messengers and construction workers. The unending symphony of cat calls were met with the standard eye roll or – in some cases – a full-on middle finger. Brice gave the few ladies he could see from where he stood an appreciative glance as the endless procession of grimy yellow cabs and buses finally came to a halt at the intersection.

The steam from two lunch specials courtesy of Hunan Wok scalded his left wrist as Brice pushed his way through the crowd of fellow pedestrians, trying to navigate between the bumpers of cars that had stopped inside the crosswalk without losing his life if a driver decided to hit the gas a moment too soon. Thankfully, he didn't have far to travel.

After crossing the street to the sidewalk, Brice took one last drag off his cigarette before flicking the butt against a brick wall and entering the airconditioned comfort of Video Star's newly carpeted entrance.

The moment he crossed the threshold and heard all the yelling, he locked eyes with his coworker and trusted neighborhood confidant Jordan "Jordie" Nash who was standing behind the checkout counter a short distance away with Gil, Jordan's father and the manager of the store. They were evidently winding down in a verbal sparring match over their favorite subject and bone of contention, the New York Rangers.

"Yeah, well...if that pretty boy Duguay hadn't gone into the box, Montreal never would've never scored the winning goal!" Gil threw his big hands up in frustration before letting them drop against his thighs. His rounded face was as red as a can of tomato soup.

"I'm *agreeing* with you!" Jordan said, his wild hand gestures matching those of his father. "So, what are you yelling at me for?" With that, Jordan turned to open the half-wall door behind the counter and rushed toward Brice.

"Jesus H. Christ!" Jordan snatched one of the bags out of Brice's hand. "It's about time! What'd you do, jump on the Circle Line to get there?" He snickered.

Brice rolled his eyes at the dramatics. "Yeah, but we sprung a leak on Second Avenue," he said, tone full of snark.

Of course, Jordan paid him no attention, already turning away with his prize. "Save me the comedy routine and grab some napkins; I'm starving."

The two headed towards the back of the store to eat. Watching them go, Gil shook his head at the boys and continued labeling a pile of clear plastic VHS boxes for the dozens of fresh bootlegs en route from the Lower East Side apartment of the store's owner, Ted. Since corporations like Blockbuster and Hollywood Video monopolized the Upper East Side neighborhood in recent years and made purchasing legit copies of new releases almost impossible, the Video Star crew was on board with a little piracy in the interest of self-preservation. Most customers were just happy to score a copy of *Beverly Hills Cop* or *The Terminator* on a Saturday night and never questioned the shaky quality or less-than-perfect resolution of the laser-printed label. A quick spin on a VCR's tracking wheel usually remedied the problem, anyway.

Ted was a math and science whiz and had been waging his own personal war against the big-box stores since they started messing with his bottom line. On one occasion, he'd managed to wipe out over two dozen of the competition's new releases with a high-powered electromagnet cleverly hidden in a briefcase. Porno rentals were a big money maker and an integral component of the store's survival; most of the big chains shied away from carrying such colorful triple X titles as *Splendor in the Ass* or *A Fist Full of Dolores*. Brice always got a kick out of restocking those.

The coast was finally clear for a quick bite. Brice and Jordan copped a squat on a few storage trunks in the back room and began to scarf down steaming plastic forkfuls of their respective meals.

Jordan's lips glistened with sesame oil and duck sauce when he turned to Brice after a few minutes. "So, what's going on with you and Lindsey?"

"Lindsey?" Brice swallowed his mouthful of fried rice with a furrowed brow. "Dude, she's like my sister!"

"I know, but she's so smoking hot with those big blue eyes and that wild red hair..." Jordan trailed off, his own eyes glazing over. Brice could guess what his friend was imagining. His own brain had gotten creative with images of himself and Lindsey in various compromising positions, but he'd stopped that a long time ago.

"I mean...yeah, we messed around a little when we were kids. I even wrote her name next to mine in bubble letters and all that jazz, but we get along much better as friends – just friends." Brice grinned and stuffed another forkful of oily rice into his mouth. "Plus, she hooks me up with all *her* friends and I hook her up with mine. I don't know if you've seen the pretties in plaid skirts she hangs out with over there at Blessed Sacrament, but every one of them is a knockout." He shrugged with one shoulder. "It's a nice arrangement. Why mess it up?"

"What about me?" Jordan's face fell as if he were legitimately put out. "*I'm* your friend!"

13

Brice rolled his eyes. Why did he have to explain the situation to his dense buddy again? He dropped his fork on the Styrofoam tray and looked Jordan in the eye to make sure he heard him well. "Really, dude? Do you not remember us having this exact conversation just last month? You know the kind of guys she goes for. I'll tell you what: as soon as you grow your hair down to your ass and start playing guitar like Eddie Van Halen, I'll mention it."

Jordan plopped back against the wall with a huff and crossed his arms. "That's fucked up."

Brice laughed and shook his head as he searched the tray in vain for one last shrimp hiding underneath a mound of fried rice.

Too soon, the unmistakable sound of the front door buzzer went off. Leaning forward, Brice spied Gil through the partially open storage room door busy preparing boxes in anticipation of Ted's arrival, so Brice put his food down and went back up front.

Brice turned toward the display cases when a jolt of electricity shot down his spine and a magnificent vision came into view.

He'd seen her a few times before, though never with a boyfriend in tow. Petite with auburn hair that flowed just past her shoulders and gleamed like silk when it caught the sunlight streaming in through the store windows. The sharp, sexy features of a femme fatale and a come-hither grin – but she wasn't offering it to Brice.

Her suitor wasn't much taller than she. He had a slender, muscular frame and chiseled bone structure, like a no-frills James Dean. The pair meandered through the few aisles before perusing the new release section.

Didn't Jordan's cousin and coworker Rex mention something about that girl before? The exact details escaped Brice at the moment. Nevertheless, it took all the strength he could muster to not get sucked in by the gravity of her allure. He had to stay professional, after all.

14

With Gil's back to the store, Brice stepped up to the counter and smiled at her when she wandered past. "Hi...can I help you find anything?"

She stopped at the sound of his voice before turning just her head to face him. A faint fluttering in the pit of Brice's stomach hit the instant their eyes met.

She approached the counter, each step unhurried, never breaking eye contact. Brice swallowed hard, his throat going dry.

"Yeah, actually. Do you have a copy of *Cobra* lying around somewhere?"

Brice had to fight the sensual shudder her smoky, Demi Moore-esque voice produced in his body. Before he could run off to find a copy of the Sylvester Stallone film, her supposed boyfriend shouted from an aisle away. "No Sly movies! That joker is a mumble-mouthed loser. He shouldn't even be making movies in the first place. We're not renting any of his shit."

Brice watched the light dim in the girl's face and felt a warm rush of anger sweep in. He remembered the impact the movie *Rocky* had had on him and his neighborhood buddies when it hit the theaters back in '76. They all wound up with their heads in the toilet after mimicking the main character's morning ritual of gulping down raw eggs in a futile attempt to jumpstart their manhood.

He could think of a few things to say to the guy to set him straight in defense of the poor girl, but he had no business getting involved in their squabble.

Instead, Brice simply cracked a fake smile, as she, her pretty face still in its fallen state, quietly said, "Um, can you find a copy of *Platoon* instead? Really quick, please."

Before he knew it, Brice was officially heated. He hated a bully,

15

and this guy was the worst kind, pushing around this beautiful, diminutive girl without even trying to hide it. He set off towards the back of the store once more to fetch the requested second title, jaw clenched tight with aggravation.

Jordan glanced up from the last of his lunch with eyes that widened at seeing the scowl on Brice's face. "Hey – what's up?" When Brice didn't answer in favor searching the scarred racks of videos lined up against the wall, Jordan set his food down and walked up front, presumably to find out for himself. After scoping out the scene and asking Gil if he needed any help, the storeroom door swung open again as Jordan returned to finish his lunch.

Brice went back to the counter with gritted teeth, the requested video in hand. This time, the pair stood before him.

He avoided looking at the boyfriend. "And what's the name on the account?"

The rat-faced prat answered for the girl, which didn't surprise Brice but pissed him off even more. "Miller. Anna Miller." He was oblivious of the fact that he'd just made a brand-new enemy.

Of course he didn't have his own account. Brice flipped through the laminated card catalogue membership file in search of last names beginning with the letter "M". He took a deep breath and tried to regain some sort of composure. His quick Brooklyn temper was hard to mask sometimes.

Brice kept his voice monotone and emotionless, even though he felt quite the opposite. "...Here. *Miller, Anna*. Okay, says here you've got a bunch of credit on file, so the charge is taken care of. This'll be due by Monday before closing or there's a late charge." He slid the video into a slick plastic bag and pushed it toward them on the counter.

"No problem," The boyfriend gave the girl a hard look. "You got that, Anna? Monday by closing."

Though Anna had hung her head and slumped her shoulders, Brice could still see the spots of red burning in her cheeks. She just nodded and turned to the door, saying nothing.

Without uttering so much as a "thank you", the guy snatched up the bag and Anna's hand before they both walked out.

Brice stood there and actually scratched his head. What kind of sorcery could have made a knockout like that fall for a zero like *that* guy?

He was just about to head into the back again when he noticed Anna looking at him through the store's front window. His heart literally stopped for a full moment when he recognized the longing in her gaze matched what he felt. Her boyfriend lit a cigarette a few feet away from her and waited for the traffic light to change. Brice cracked a smile as he and Anna locked eyes for a split second. Then the crosswalk light turned green and within an instant they both were swallowed by the crowd.

Brice stood frozen for a minute, basking in the lingering warmth of that brief moment and trying to shake off the remains of his residual anger.

"What the hell was that all about?" Jordan gave Brice an expectant stare when Brice finally returned to the storeroom and his lunch, though now the once tasty fried rice had the same culinary appeal as an old dish rag.

Brice moved his takeout tray aside and heaved a sigh. "I don't know, man. How does a jerkoff like that get his hooks into a sweetheart like her?" He took a deep breath before he continued. "What's her story again? I think Rex kind of told me once, but I forgot."

Jordan pursed his lips in thought for a second, then scratched his narrow chin. "Her dad was Garland Miller, I think."

17

It didn't ring a bell for Brice. "Okay, and what did Garland Miller do that made him such a big deal?"

"He wrote the screenplay and score for that show *Bombshells over Broadway* and a bunch of other really famous stuff, too." Jordan began lazily pushing back his cuticles with a thumbnail.

Brice's eyes bucked at the news. "Wow, really? That is a pretty big deal, huh?"

"Yep." Jordan leaned back against the wall, folded his hands over his belly, and closed his eyes with a contented sigh.

Brice leaned back as well but found he was far too wired for a nap. "Oh, man...what's the song from that show they play all the time at Christmas? "Spring Summer" or something?"

Jordan spoke without opening his eyes. "'You Spring Summer on Me and I Fall for It every Winter'."

Brice grinned. "That's the one! Jesus Christ, you can't go ten minutes without hearing that damn tune between December and January. Man, they must be rich as The Rothschilds, huh?"

"I guess so," Jordan said on a chuckle. "You can't live in this neighborhood and not be."

Getting up, Brice threw the oily remnants of his midday meal into the large open trash can close to the rear exit and returned to his post.

Brice caught his boss' eye as he grabbed a labeled plastic bag from the stack on the far end of the counter. "Hey, Gil – I'm going to run this delivery over to Regent Hospital. I need a little fresh air."

Gil nodded over his shoulder and continued working on the mountain of empty video cases.

Brice hit the streets to clear his head, annoyed with himself for being so easily triggered. It had been a really tough year. Getting kicked out of his Catholic high school had made him feel like he couldn't do anything right, and honestly, he still didn't feel worth a damn, barely getting by at his new school. His home life felt shaky as well, with him alternating between staying with his mom, aunt and uncle and grandmother, no real place to call his own. Not that his family didn't love him or want him around, but...there were way more downs than ups in his life as of late. Brice had never felt so out of place, like he didn't belong. He had no clue what he wanted his future to look like, but after meeting Anna today, he did have a better idea of who he wanted to be in it.

The space between adolescence and adulthood sure was a complicated intersection to navigate. Something eventually had to give. Alice Cooper's song "Eighteen", really hit the nail on the head of how Brice felt.

I'm in the middle without any plans...I'm a boy and I'm a man...

The song rang out in his head as Brice faded into the hustle and bustle of the noisy metropolis.

CHAPTER 2

The lingering shock waves from the afternoon bell bounced off the penitentiary-gray walls as Brice and a sea of restless teens made their way through halls and out of the exits of Fort Brambleton High School.

"The Bramble", as it was called, was built in the mid-1930s and acted as an architectural and educational time capsule – a living fossil of the New York City public school system. A few faculty members had actually been there since the end of World War Two. Other than the occasional quick fix or plaster job, the building hadn't changed much since its original construction. Desks, gymnasium bleachers and furnishings were all still original and encased in a drab cocoon of lead paint and asbestos.

Brice had his guitar case and books in hand when he spotted his comrades in arms. Max, Evan, and the rest of the crew were all lighting up cigarettes and hanging tough by the basketball courts.

It was still hard for Brice to believe that less than a year ago he and Max were three years deep into a private college preparatory program courtesy of St. Ignatius School for Boys. Brooklyn's premier parochial academy only accepted a handful of top performing students every year. He, Max and Evan had scored unexpectedly well on the entrance exams and were admitted. Never ones for spending too much time on any of that pesky book-learning, their luck finally ran out after a series of disciplinary incidents and subpar grades rendered them ineligible to proceed on to senior year. Without any chances for a last minute reprieve, they were forced to "Ramble over to the Bramble" for senior year.

Evan, with the size and stature of a young professional wrestler, had been handed his hat from the academy one year prior. He was the heir apparent to his dad's arcade and vending machine empire, and didn't catch much heat when his academic "Dear John" letter arrived in the mail. His old man had only made it to the eighth grade and was more concerned with his son taking over the reins of the family business and making a decent buck.

Brice approached the group. Max, a world champion wise-ass, looked at Brice's guitar case and cracked a wide grin tossing a fresh Marlboro Red in Brice's direction. "What's up, rock star? You still telling all the chicks in history class you actually know how to play that thing?"

Catching the cigarette against his chest, Brice laughed and fell back a step. "You know it, man! We can't all get by on our good looks." Max was a deadringer for a young Matt Dillon, with criminally high cheek bones and the coolest shag haircut known to man. "But if they ever actually ask me to play something, I'll be up shit's creek!"

The boys burst into laughter and Brice slapped palms with Evan and the rest of the squad. After finding a seat, Brice finished up his flip-click-light-and-shut routine with his cigarette and prized chrome Zippo lighter and exhaled a long plume of smoke before turning back to Max. "Hey, are we still doing the roadie thing for your brother at LeRoxx on Friday?" Seducer's Charm, fronted by Max's big brother Grant, was the hottest local band in the neighborhood and had quickly made a name for themselves in the tri-state area club scene.

Max nodded. "Yeah, buddy. Charlotte's Web is headlining, so you know the place is gonna be packed!" He raised an eyebrow at Brice. "Hey, make sure you invite Lindsey and her merry maidens to the after party at HQ! My folks are gonna be away in the Poconos."

10 Bay Crest Court – or "HQ", as it was lovingly nicknamed – was a modest two-story Brooklyn brownstone situated on a quiet cobblestone street. Complete with stained glass windows and a thick blanket of ivy creeping up the outside walls, the unassuming abode was home to Max, Grant, and their parents, Bill and Grace. Their parents were just a few years away from retirement and regularly spent most weekends at their vacation cottage nestled

deep in the Pocono Mountains.

At a glance, one would never suspect that the quaint residence had hosted some of the most legendary rock and roll after parties in the entire neighborhood. The main floor, with its rustic exposed brick walls, was tastefully adorned with antiques and family portraits dating back to the late 1800s. The back of the house held the dining area that looked over an immaculately manicured garden. That was where resident rock and roll god Grant would hold court with his personal stash of Parliament Lights and frosty cans of Meister Brau beer, all bought on a revolving line of credit thanks to Big Lou at the corner deli.

Grant caught the performing bug early and was fronting bands by the tender age of thirteen. He and whatever group he was in at the time would play any dive bar or function that would have them. As kids, Max, Brice, and Evan would sneak down to the basement to watch rehearsals every chance they got. With his bright orange hip huggers, tube top and a vintage Les Paul slung way down low, Grant was a force to be reckoned with and quickly gained the respect of all the older musicians in the neighborhood who simply referred to him as "The Kid".

Brice slipped his lighter back in his leather jacket's inside pocket, flipping up both thumbs like Fonzie circa 1978 before taking another deep drag of his smoke. Max's suggestion was a good time if Brice had ever heard one. He took another deep drag and gave him a lopsided grin. "I'm on it!"

Evan, ever the ball-buster, walked over and tapped Brice on the back of his head before assuming his usual faux fighting stance.

Brice chuckled. "C'mon, bro...you really want me to have to school your big dumb ass in front of everybody?"

Evan grimaced with feigned disapproval and playfully backed off. "I'll let you slide this time, punk, but know this: you've been warned."

Brice and the others nearly fell over laughing. It took a while for everyone to calm down.

Over his shoulder, Max waved goodbye to two of the group's heavily eyelined female counterparts, flicked his cigarette over the fence, then leveled a questioning stare at Brice. "So, what's your story now? Are you still living over at your mom's full time or your aunt and uncle's? I can't keep track anymore."

Brice flicked his cigarette butt over the fence in kind and sighed, shoulder muscles tightening. He didn't want to talk about it, but Max was a good friend. "Dude, I don't even really know anymore. I just kind of bounce back and forth between both places and crash at Granny's from time to time. I'm like a fucking wandering gypsy." Brice kept his eyes on the horizon, burning with teen angst. He hated feeling that way, but there seemed to be no help for it. "My mother's still bent out of shape about me getting kicked out of St. Ig's. My aunt and uncle aren't any less bummed out about it, but they don't constantly bring it up. And then when I can't take either place, I go and crash at my grandmother's place. She sits in her chair knitting and listening to Eydie Gorme' records while I catch up on sleep and soak up all her positive vibes."

Brice shrugged and posed his rebuttal to Max. "How come your folks don't break your balls about getting the boot? You fucked things up just as bad as I did!"

Max cocked his head in thought for a minute. "I guess they're just worn out after all the shit they've been through with Grant. They probably figure what's done is done and are hoping for the best. I mean, I'm still in school and gainfully employed at the record store. What more do they want?"

Brice nodded. Good point. Too bad it didn't apply to Brice's life. "Yeah, well, I've got a completely different type of situation going on."

Principal Feld walked over then with bullhorn in hand, balding head shining in the sun beneath a cringe worthy comb-over that resembled bacon strips. He turned to the group and shook his head before shouting into the bullhorn. "C'mon, folks—chop-chop! Let's start moving! School is officially over for the day. Don't you people spend enough time in this place, for Christ's sake? I know I sure as shit do." Brice caught the last bit the man mumbled to himself as the crowd of students finally started to disperse.

****

Later that afternoon at Video Star, a few customers in fancy footwear were aimlessly perusing the shelves for something worth the $4.99 rental fee as owner Ted typed away feverishly on the store's brand new IBM computer, purchased for a real steal for only $4,799. He'd sworn that was cheap, but Brice had almost fainted when he'd heard the price. The stacks of perforated printer paper covered in infinite streams of undecipherable character symbols offered no clue of how close Ted was coming to creating a program that could help him beat the gambling odds in Atlantic City – he was a fiend for Black Jack, and his penchant for card counting had landed him an escort off casino property more than once. Brice had let his mind go numb and quiet for a while rewinding tapes when he heard the door buzzer go off. He raised his head to see Anna Miller approaching the counter, and the same warm rush he felt the last time they'd locked eyes coursed through him again. She looked insanely beautiful in her lavender sundress, tan cowboy boots, denim jacket and wayfarer shades.

She was a big Stallone fan; Brice could just act kind of like Sly in *The Lords of Flatbush* without going too overboard. There was a thin line between cool and fool.

He cocked his head to the side and said, "Hey you. How'd you like Platoon?" Anna grimaced. "Oh, my God! It was so horrible. I only watched like ten minutes and went to bed." She paused to glance around the room before making eye contact again, her lighthearted tone becoming more a serious one. She looked up at Brice through her lashes. "Hey, listen...I want to apologize for how rude my

24

boyfriend was acting the other day. He can be a real jerk sometimes."

The urge to tell her he completely agreed bubbled up in Brice's chest, but he immediately tamped it down. He waited a few seconds before he spoke, trying to give his brain time to say something sensible and calm. Anna looked like a million and a half bucks in that outfit and he could feel himself starting to get a little revved up.

He put on a sympathetic face and said instead, "No worries. He must have just been having a bad day. It happens to all of us."

Anna brushed her hair over her shoulder and smiled at him, emerald eyes gleaming bright as the day outside. The floor seemed to disappear beneath Brice's feet and he had to subtly lean against the counter for support.

He wasn't sure if she noticed, but a faint blush stained her cheeks before she averted her stare and looked up at the wall of tapes behind him that stood ten feet high. "Anyway, thanks for being so nice. I wanted to see if you guys had a copy of *Evil Dead* in, because part two is going to be coming out in the theaters in the next few weeks."

As a huge horror fan himself, this new tidbit of slasher flick intel took Brice aback. He'd heard no news of such an important cinematic event. "Really? *Evil Dead Two*!?" He shook his head in disbelief. "Are you sure?"

Full of confidence, Anna nodded. "I'm positive."

Brice grinned at the thought of getting a new dose of his beloved kitschy blood-and-guts franchise. He busied himself locating the title she asked for when he said over his shoulder, "You don't strike me as the low-budget horror flick type." He winced the instant the words left his mouth. God, he hoped she didn't take that the wrong way, that he'd thought she was a snob or something.

When he dared to peek back at her, Anna gave him a sideways

grin like she'd been waiting for him to look at her. "Well, you shouldn't make that kind of an assumption before you get to know a person."

Was...was that an invitation to do just that? Brice's stomach was doing summersaults at the prospect of getting to know the heavenly creature standing behind him. Not looking at her – and frankly, not daring to with how he felt – he snorted a soft laugh. "You have a point." Brice located and retrieved the title, then pulled out an invoice pad and started thumbing through the membership files. "Okay...Miller, right? Miller. Hmm. Where could it...?"

He trailed off and hoped Anna didn't catch that he'd done so quite purposefully. The transaction and conversation would be over in a few seconds. Desperate times called for desperate measures.

Brice gave her a long look through narrowed, curious eyes. "Hey, any relation to Garland Miller? You kinda look like him, to tell the truth." Talk about playing dirty cards!

Anna's jaw dropped. "Wow–yeah, Garland Miller's my dad. Well, he was my dad. He died when I was like six." She put a hand on her hip. "Most people under seventy have never even heard of him. I'm impressed!" Brice smiled, no longer feeling the least bit of guilt for bringing up her past. Still, he kept his tone light and casual. "Yeah, I know who he was. Super talented guy! Sorry you lost him at such a young age. I lost my dad when I was about two, so I can totally relate."

As Anna offered her condolences, Brice thanked her then continued writing. When he chuckled under his breath, Anna grinned again and raised her eyebrows. "What's so funny?"

"Oh, I was just thinking about that tune from one of your dad's shows that they play every year around the holidays. It goes into heavy rotation on Thanksgiving and then on New Year's Day? *Poof* – it vanishes".

26

Anna laughed, a sultry exhalation. Even that was sexy. "Yeah, no matter how much they play it, people still seem to love it."

"Some things just hold up over time, I guess." Knowing he couldn't draw this out any longer without seeming like a weirdo, Brice placed the tape and order slip into its plastic bag and said "Well, you're all set. I hope this tides you over until you get to see the sequel."

Brice held out his hand with the bag. As Anna reached up and grabbed it, time stood still as they locked eyes once again, and it was just as potent as the first time. If not more. Brice didn't pull away...but neither did she, even when it was far past the point that one of them should have.

Finally Anna, with bag in hand, put on her shades and offered up a big heartfelt "thank you". She pointed right at Brice. "Now, remember: if you wind up seeing it first, I don't want to hear a word about it. No spoilers, okay?"

Brice raised his right hand and looked as serious as he could. "Scout's honor."

Anna smirked and gave him a sideways look. "You weren't a Boy Scout, were you?"

That was beside the point, wasn't it? Brice laughed. "Get going, you little troublemaker, and enjoy your movie." He took one final look at her as she opened the door and walked off. Ted just looked up from his computer and chuckled before going back to his numbers.

CHAPTER 3

The line outside LeRoxx nightclub snaked halfway around the block as muffled sounds from the club's 2000-watt sound system throbbed mercilessly out into the street.

Clouds of hairspray and cheap perfume hung heavy in the air, choking Brice, Max and Evan as they filed out of a battered rental van and proceeded to unload all of Seducer's gear. Grant and the band's guitarist, Rolly, started barking orders at the trio like drill sergeants. LeRoxx ran a tight ship, especially for local opener bands that hadn't yet been handed the golden ring of rock stardom. Loading in and out were always stressful endeavors.

The club's stage supervisor known simply as "Tiny" – towering over the tallest in the band at nearly seven feet tall and weighing an easy 350 pounds – waved the boys through with arms covered in tattoos through the load-in entrance with a stern glance. Brice and the boys had been at this long enough now that despite the clock ticking down to show time, the amplifiers, guitars and the group's 19-piece candy apple red drum kit complete with a brass gong were assembled with pinpoint accuracy.

A little while later, the shrill cry of electric guitars on the main stage heralded the start of the evening's event. Brice finished hanging up the group's Cobra-emblazoned gong and peeked out from behind the thick velvet stage curtain. He let out a primal scream into the crowd to help get things going and caught the attention of Lindsey and her constant companions, Eva and Sherri. All of them were dressed to impress in their too-short skirts, ripped denim and leather, makeup applied so thickly Brice could see their glittery eye shadow and pink cheeks from the stage. Lindsey flashed him the two-finger devil's horn, ready to rock out full tilt.

Brice laughed aloud and turned to the others as they finished up.

"Hey gents, the ladies have arrived."

Max grinned at the news; Evan made an obscene hand gesture and giggled like a child. With their tasks complete, all three bolted off the stage to hang out with the girls in the crowd of glammed-out Brooklyn headbangers getting ready to let loose.

Twenty minutes later, Seducer's Charm was grinding through a blistering set of high-energy rock and roll as an army of glittering guys and dolls pumped their fists with every crackling snare drum hit. Heavy white smoke billowed out from under the stage as shards of multicolored neon light danced against the haze. Brice, Max and Evan didn't have the luxury of enjoying the show. Adrenal glands pumping, they stood at the ready on opposite sides of the stage to keep a watchful eye out for any equipment or instrument malfunction that would warrant an immediate response.

Brice checked out the crowd and dug the scene. Grant glowed like a shaman from the lights shining up from the stage. He held the crowd in the palm of his leather-gloved hands as he slithered and gyrated across the stage like a serpent. Years spent studying the moves of heavyweights like Roger Daltry, Mick Jagger and David Lee Roth had paid dividends, culminating in effortless stage prowess. Headliners Charlotte's Web tried in vain to keep a low profile; the whole band stood off in a corner studying the scene and taking mental notes from the sidelines. Seducer's Charm managed to be a tough act to follow. Judging by the dejected looks on their faces, the Web boys knew on this particular night, they were going to have to go big or go home.

Brice caught a glimpse of Lindsey and her crew shoulder to shoulder with all of the other sweaty party goers, wild-eyed and jubilant. Jordan's remarks that week at the video store came to mind as Brice watched the girls. He and Lindsey would make a cool couple. Back in second grade she had been his first real crush, complete with feeble attempts at holding hands and promises of a Friday night date at the local pizzeria. It seemed like yesterday when John Seever screamed, "Hey, Lindsey! Brice likes you!" across the

P.S. 108 school yard. After a brief fling in the eighth grade, Brice and Lindsay agreed that they would be friends above all else, with a secret pact that if they both found themselves unattached near the end of their twenties, they would indeed pursue a more romantic path resulting in nuptials, kids and all of the other mundane trappings of a traditional domestic union.

Reality rushed back in as Rolly, having just broken a low E string, flashed a desperate look and motioned for Brice to come and remedy the situation. With reflexes like a cat, Brice grabbed a Telecaster from the band's guitar rack and jetted stealthily behind the wall of amplifiers. Without missing a beat, the replacement was soon in Rolly's capable hands, ringing out for all to hear.

Brice slinked back to his designated spot at stage left, slapped the wounded six-string back in the rack and waited for the next mishap to unfold. Grant looked over and gave him a big sideways smile with a nod of approval. Max and Evan never passed up a chance to bust Brice's chops; they both feigned adoration and gave their comrade a limp-wristed applause, which Brice immediately met with an enthusiastic middle finger.

Luckily, the rest of the show went off without a hitch. After a double encore – almost unheard of for an opening act – Brice, Max and Evan broke down the band's equipment and had it loaded back into the van by the time Charlotte's Web struck their first chord.

Back in the crowd and fully enjoying the sonic ruckus at last, Brice and the boys scanned the sea of heavily rouged faces for a certain someone that possessed the necessary chemical compound needed to round out the evening's after party festivities.

Robert Feeney Jr. – or "Bob Rock", as he was called - was a New York City transit worker built like an old fridge with bad acne and an equally terrible haircut. He got his nickname for the quality bricks of pure white cocaine he peddled. Bob had been admitted into the Seducer's Charm inner circle solely for the fact that he allowed band members and their friends to buy grams of his magic marching powder mostly on credit. As a bonus, Bob had a habit of getting completely hammered on shots and his own stash, causing him to fall way short of keeping accurate tabs on who'd purchased what.

After collecting the necessary funding from all who were planning on jamming a tightly rolled dollar bill up their noses at HQ, the trio made their way to the nook next to the DJ booth where Bob was busy chatting up a few honeys in stilettos. Under normal circumstances, these stunners wouldn't let a guy like him wash their cars for free, but in this scene on a Friday night, cocaine was the magic key that unlocked doors which would otherwise remain impenetrable.

The management at LeRoxx was an extremely tough bunch with ties to organized crime. Transactions like this one had to be carried out quickly and quietly. Bouncers could be dispatched at a moment's notice to dole out instant justice to troublemakers and anybody else bringing unwanted attention. The local police precinct was paid a handsome monthly fee to look the other way for most things, but they would only tolerate so much.

Dazzle, the cocktail waitress in her zebra print miniskirt, floated around the room and was immediately flagged down by a colorful group of rockers eager to drown themselves in diluted tequila shots and warm cans of beer for five dollars a pop.

Bob was preoccupied with his curvy gal pals but caught a glimpse of Max, Evan and Brice eagerly waiting to do business. In under a minute, they exchanged legal tender for illegal splendor.

With the wax paper rectangle now clenched tightly in his fist, Max grinned back at Evan and Brice. Brice knew that smile – Bob had given them a prime picking from his friends and family stack. Most dealers cut their dope heavily with baby laxatives or powered milk to increase the weight and profits, but Max, being Grant's kid brother, always got taken care of like a prince.

31

CHAPTER 4

The same brand of high-octane rock that carried on into the night over at LeRoxx was now wailing out of Grant's hi-fi speakers as the evening's revelers started pouring in through the doors of HQ. With Grant and Max's folks now tucked in their beds two solid hours away in their mountain chalet, the coast was clear for an evening of debauchery and mischief. Spandex, leather, spikes and lace were all on full display as the caustic scents of weed and cigarette smoke filled the air. Brice and his buddies scoped out the scene, trying to make eye contact with every chick that wasn't already on the arm of some dandy.

Well, at least Max and Evan were. All Brice could think about was Anna and the fat gram of blow they'd just copped from Bob. He leaned closer to Max and laid out his plan. "So, why don't we cut up a few lines like right away, and then kinda ration it out as the night goes on? After everybody's done smoking up what we've got left of this Slunky's bag and sucking down a case of brews, how much more fucked up can we get?"

Always one to listen to reason, Max nodded in agreement. In addition to being the neighborhood's premier rehearsal space for rock stars in training, Slunky Studios sold the best weed in the neighborhood. For a mere 20 dollars, a group could spend an evening smoking themselves straight and then back up to high as a kite while barely making a dent in the tin foil-wrapped stalk of stinky mulch.

Brice chuckled and said, "Oh, dude; I forgot to tell you. This is so funny...I spent like an hour last week cutting holes into this old, faded pair of jeans before I hit the club. Anyway, I crashed at my grandmother's place afterwards because I hadn't seen her in a while. Dude, when I got up, she'd sewn back up *every single* hole in my jeans. It was like surgeon had snuck in while I was sleeping. She really missed her calling as a ringside stitch man."

32

Max burst out laughing. "Get out!"

Brice, feeling the relaxing effect of the weed, shrugged and laughed so hard himself he could barely speak. "I swear! I couldn't fucking believe it. It must have taken her all night! She goes, 'I thought you didn't have any money for new clothes'. She's too cute. Go Gramms! How could I possibly get mad at her?"

Max slapped him on the shoulder, still chuckling. "That's fucking great!"

The hypnotic drums and rhythm guitars of Led Zeppelin's "Kashmir" had just begun to flood the room as Brice spied Lindsey and her posse strutting through the front door. Lindsey's fiery red hair always caused a stir. Every dude within eye shot almost broke their necks trying to get a good look. She somehow managed to find the exact shade of red lipstick to perfectly match her hair. Eva and Sherri were no slouches either and usually commanded the unwavering attention of any young man with a functioning set of eyes.

Evan, having already downed a six-pack by himself with a pair of mystery blue pills his cousin gave him, was beginning to slur his words. Brice watched him catch sight of the newly arrived trio and stumble over to greet them. Brice followed in case he needed to help his friend off the floor.

With the fake charm of a cheesy Manhattan maître'd, Evan grabbed Eva's hand and said, "Welcome, ladies. I'm so glad you could join us this evening. I trust you found the place without any trouble."

Max laughed like Evan's antics were the funniest thing he'd ever witnessed. "Dude, what the fuck are you talking about? They're here almost every other weekend!"

Evan was clearly obliterated at this point. He giggled hysterically and flipped Max the bird before reaching into his denim jacket pocket for a tightly rolled bone of Mexico's finest. Without missing a beat, Brice produced his lighter with its dramatically oversized flame and offered it to him.

Within a few seconds, the joint was put into heavy rotation. A thick cloud of pungent cheeba rose up along the low hanging ceiling and back down the wood paneled walls. Between deep hits and subsequent coughing like a tuberculosis patient, Max told the tale of the early days before Slunky's started peddling weed, when the ever enterprising Evan would risk his neck to go deep into the Puerto Rican part of town to cop the cheapest dog shit herb around, only to cut up a dime bag with some of his mother's Earl Grey tea and oregano then peddling his wares to their crowd of tween peers for three to four bucks a joint.

The party at HQ was now in full swing. Max chuckled upon hearing the familiar sound of Grant's gravelly, post-show voice wafting out of the dining room as he began yet another rendition of his legendary Randy Rhodes story to his best bro Tristan, girlfriend Dana, and a fresh set of eager young ears gathering around the great oak table. Max and Evan lead Lindsey and her pals to an unoccupied area of the living room, Brice trailing behind them.

Record cover in hand, the group hunkered down and began the painstaking process of cutting up lines. Shit-faced Evan insisted on performing the carving duties. Brice looked at Max, glad the decision wasn't his to make since Evan had chipped in more than anyone in the group.

Max handed Evan the small, shiny package. "Be very fucking careful, bro," he said in warning as Evan marveled at the square. He held it up to his runny nose and breathed it in. Evan reached into his jacket and pulled out his expired St. Ignatius identification card before dumping out a pile of coke onto the record cover. Brice glanced up at Lindsey and Max while Evan went to work. The two of them seemed to be digging each other's company a bit more than usual. They'd always had an on-again, off-again thing that depended mostly on if either of them had plans of hooking up with someone else.

It didn't bother Brice. He and everyone else in the circle started to relax as the mid tempo throb of Judas Priest's "Victim of Changes" echoed throughout the house. Brice and Max kept a close eye on Evan as he clumsily whacked the blow into comical, asymmetrical rails. Given the exorbitant cost, it was painful to watch, but breaking his balls at this point would be pointless.

It was agreed that in the interest of chivalry and the unspoken slim chance of one of the guys getting laid, the ladies would go first. They rolled their eyes in unison as Evan thought it absolutely necessary to give a longwinded preamble before the games began.

The girls were getting noticeably perturbed as he proudly informed them that every time the group cut up the blow, it was on the same album cover: Max's mom's coveted copy of Frank Sinatra's "She Shot Me Down". Clumsily, he tried to hold it up to show them, sending an avalanche of white powder cascading onto his lap as Brice and Max lunged forward to try and mitigate the unforgivable blunder. Max ordered him not to move an inch until further notice. Thankfully, his corduroy trousers managed to catch and hold the precious blow. They sniffed the folds of fabric clean for the next hour.

CHAPTER 5

Brice's head throbbed as the Saturday morning sun crept through HQ's small basement windows. If those walls could talk, no one would ever believe a word of it.

Max and Lindsey lay entwined on the floor next Evan and the other girls, all of whom were snoring like chainsaws. Brice eased himself off the floor with great effort and crept up the rickety stairs to the main floor. As he turned the corner, he caught a glimpse of Grant sitting in the exact same spot and wearing last night's stage clothes. In the morning light, he looked like a regal rock and roll sage. Dana and the rest of the evening's casualties lay strewn about on the living room couches and loveseats.

As Brice walked out of the front door he turned back at the last second, clicked his heels, and saluted Grant, who raised up a fresh can of beer in thanks for a job well done at the show. "When my ship comes in, buddy, you're all coming along for the ride," Grant called to Brice down the long hallway, heedless of the remaining party guests that still slept all over the house. Getting signed and making it to the big leagues was a long shot, but Brice honestly believed that if it ever did happen, Grant would keep his word.

Now out on the street, Brice walked towards his mom's place to get ready for work. The morning air felt fresh and clean, sweeping the stale party fumes from his lungs. Old ladies in kerchiefs and shopping carts gave him and his rumpled clothes dirty looks as they headed up to the avenue in search of good deals on Entenmann's crumb cake and panty hose.

Though he went straight to his room to clean up the moment he stepped into the house, Brice still found his mother waiting for him in her bathrobe when he walked out of the bathroom still steamy from his quick shower. With a towel around his waist and a toothbrush in his mouth, Brice knew he was in for an earful. He tried to make sense out of the battery of words spilling out a mile a minute.

"So, I went up to school and met with your English teacher yesterday!" Her brown eyes practically glowed red as she crossed her arms and stared up at him.

Well, that didn't sound good. How had he not known about it? "Why?"

His mother held up a piece of paper and put it directly in front of his face for him to see. "Because she sent me a letter – yeah, a nice handwritten one, too! She looked me right in the eye and said, 'if he doesn't get his act together, I'm going to fail him, graduation or not'."

Brice's head sank but his stomach sank even lower. That was not the kind of news he wanted to hear early on a Saturday morning.

She thumped her finger right into his chest bone and said, "Listen – you'd better start buckling down, mister. You have less than three months left until graduation. Okay? Do you really want to have to go to summer school or even worse: have to repeat another half year?"

Brice sighed through his nose and looked everywhere but at her. The insane fun of the night before already felt like a lifetime ago. "No" he said, not bothering to raise his head as shame settled over him like a soaking wet blanket.

His mom dropped her arms. "Then get serious and get this over with. You can do whatever you want after you graduate, but you have to graduate. Understand?"

Brice nodded and walked back to his room, leaving his mother in the hallway in a frustrated huff. There was nothing else to say.

Saturday mornings at Video Star were a kaleidoscopic spectacle of organized chaos and Upper East Side snobbery. Customers crammed into what could only be described as a shoe box to rent, return, peruse, schmooze and generally complain that they'd "seen everything".

It was usually all hands on deck – and what a colorful deck it was. Gil worked full time all week to take Saturdays off and had Jordan come in on the weekends in his place. Daisy, a sassy Puerto Rican chick from Spanish Harlem who made Rosie Perez sound like an Oxford trained thespian, usually handled tape putaways and deliveries while Jordan's cousin Rex impressed customers with his extensive knowledge of art house and foreign films. Arrogance was his forte and it was not unusual to hear him belittle customers in one breath whilst subtly peddling his canvases of personal fine art.

Everyone from old money billionaires, A-list entertainers, sportscasters, and diplomats all walked through the doors of Video Star to scour over their extensive collection of titles. At least three or four times a year the store would get a call from the very exclusive Plaza Athanee's Hotel's concierge with a request for a dozen or so titles for "you know who" – Sir Paul McCartney and his wife, Linda. Under normal circumstances, a sampler platter of new releases consisting of comedies, dramas, action flicks and the like would be scooped up and sent over. With Sir Paul, however, there was a special set of requirements: no titles containing any off-colored humor, animal cruelty, racism, sexism or a myriad of life's other unpleasantries.

This proved to be a daunting task and usually required a group effort, typically resulting in Brice using a choice selection of pejoratives directed at a certain Liverpudlian who wasn't emotionally capable of handling the realities of life and Jordan, a diehard Fab Four fan, giving him a big pass. "He's a Beatle bro....a frigging Beatle" was all he'd say to Brice's complaints.

Then there were the oddballs, misfits whose obscene bank accounts and social standing in the upper echelon of society allowed them to live their lives with little awareness of how off the wall they were to the average Joe. Lori Bandasarian was the crown jewel of this lot. Second in line to a vast real estate fortune which included the building Video Star resided at, her dark Armenian Jewish features, Jackie-O sunglasses and outrageous outfits only added to the spectacle of her Tourette's-like outbursts in the store. Ted, usually a month or two behind on the rent at any given time, made it very clear to all that she could do, say or request anything at any time without reproach.

The second in line to the oddity throne was Henry Krauss, also known as "Der Fuhrer" – a befitting moniker, compliments of Gil. While Michael Douglas' character Gordon Gekko was busy pretending to rape and pillage his way through publicly traded companies in the movie *Wall Street*, Henry's company, Krauss Holdings Limited was actually generating incredible profits leveraging and liquidating assets of vulnerable NASDAQ companies. Henry was a raging alcoholic and borderline schizophrenic. At the behest of his board of directors and big money backers, he was ordered to work from home.

For reasons unknown, he took a shining to Brice and made it clear that only he was permitted to make deliveries to his plush Park Avenue digs. Henry's building had an old fashioned elevator complete with its own operator who worked the archaic levers and gears with the grace and elegance of a concert pianist. Brice was usually greeted at the door by his assistant. Though pleasantly soft spoken, she was a tall, thin hag of a woman with bad skin and turquoise hair twisted into a braid at the base of her neck. From there, she lead Brice into the hallway to meet Henry in his ratty terrycloth robe and cocktail in one hand, who always grabbed the bag of tapes from Brice's hands as if it were a sack of takeout that was an hour overdue. Then the short, fat, unshaven brute would berate Brice for wasting his young life working at some rinky dink video rental shop instead of trying his hand in the stock and bonds business.

With the morning rush now behind them, Brice and Jordan took a breather outside, admiring all well-kept ladies as they strolled by in a steady flow of finely coiffed loveliness. Brice looked into the store, shook his head and chuckled. "Dude, your cousin Rex is a real trip.

39

He works here like two days a week and acts like he fucking owns the joint."

Jordan smirked. "I know. He's been signing off on free club renewals without anyone's permission. He just writes 'see Rex'. And how about him trying to sell his paintings to customers? Ted's this close to canning his ass. If he wasn't my dad's nephew, he'd have already been gone."

Brice kicked a discarded soda can into the street. Even a video rental store wasn't immune to nepotism in this city. "Yeah, he's a total kook, but dude, I've seen the way he operates. There's no denying that chicks dig him. It must be that starving artist vibe or something. I know for a fact he's banging that one super fine broad. What's her name? Evelyn? The blonde that comes in with the kid. She's got some gazillionaire keeping her set up in a luxury pad and ol' Rexy gets to swing by whenever he wants to 'service the account'. Crazy, huh?"

Feeling a few rain drops falling on his head, Brice didn't wait for Jordan to respond. "Okay, I'm going back in." He paused for second. "I guess we're taking the subway back tonight since your pops ain't working today. Right?"

Jordan shrugged and kept watching the busy street, distracted by a darkhaired girl that smiled at him. "That's the plan, Stan."

With the store locked up tighter than Fort Knox at closing time, Jordan and Brice caught the express train back to Brooklyn. A bum entered their car and started laying his sob story on the clearly unsympathetic crowd. They all quickly looked away so as not to offer him any false hopes of a donation.

Jordan rubbed his temples and said, "Damn, I'm exhausted."

Brice nodded in agreement, his own head beginning to throb. "Man, me too. And I gotta work tomorrow!"

Jordan cringed. "I hate working on Sundays. Though it's nice clocking those extra ducats, right?"

It was indeed, but it would have been even nicer to not have to work the weekend to get them. "Hey man, did you ever wonder what it would be like to live up by the store? Can you imagine having so much money you never have to worry about anything?"

Jordan snorted. "What made you think about that?"

"I made a delivery the other day up to Madison Avenue. This lady's apartment took up the entire fourth floor, bro. I stepped off the elevator and it was like I was standing in the middle of the Taj Mahal. It blew my mind!" Brice couldn't stop thinking about that beautiful place long after he'd left.

Jordan just shrugged. "I try not to think about it too much. I guess if you're born into it, it's not a big deal. I'm pretty sure the money alone wouldn't buy you happiness. Most of our customers walk around looking just as miserable as everyone in Brooklyn. They just have bigger bank accounts and nicer apartments."

Brice laughed at his buddy's sardonic take and said, "Yeah, but still. Just once I'd like to see what the view's like from the inside looking out."

The two closed their eyes until the conductor announced their arrival and Atlantic Avenue station for the local connection.

CHAPTER 6

Brice dragged his aching bones through the front door of yet another family home and was greeted by his Aunt Maggie. She pinched his cheek and shouted over her shoulder. "Amir, Brice is home! Take out the *mishwi* and the ratatouille!" Already smiling, Brice heard his enthusiastic "Okay!" from the kitchen.

"How's my beamish boy?" she asked as Brice took off his jacket and handed it to her. Removing it somehow felt like taking off a lead weight he'd had slung over his shoulders.

"Dog tired," he said, and wasn't that the truth. But he was already feeling a little better. Aunt Maggie was his father's sister and had provided a safe and loving environment all his life. In the last year, she became a godsend given the tumultuous nature of Brice's life. They had a nice house a few blocks away from the Narrows with a big back yard which was a nice change of pace from the daily confines of living in a small apartment. Though always concerned about his wellbeing and future, Brice had never known her to push the questioning of his choices too far. He appreciated that more than she'd ever know.

Uncle Amir appeared from the kitchen and wrapped Brice in a hug that smelled of warm spices and cooked lamb. Brice's mouth instantly began to water. "How was work today? Did any movie stars come in?" His uncle's thick Lebanese accent gave a lilt to every vowel he spoke.

Brice just grinned at the usual inquiry he heard every time he came home. "Not today, Unc."

Brice went upstairs to his room and made a few phone calls before dinner. Max and Evan were pretty much DOA after their Friday night escapades and had both gone to bed early. On the other hand,

Lindsey was always the party animal and chatted away about nothing in particular while applying her makeup to hit the clubs again with her gal pals. Brice heard her mother in the background asking if she needed her mini skirt ironed and laughed out loud. Lindsey got Brice up to speed on all the scene gossip in a few minutes – what bands were playing where next, who'd slept with whom, etc. With his stomach growling painfully, he signed off with her and cleaned up for dinner.

Seated at the dinner table with his family, Brice breathed in the steaming bowl of Middle Eastern goodness before tearing off a hunk of pita bread beside his bowl and stuffing his face. He moaned with appreciation when the spices and rich sauce hit his tongue. Uncle Amir was truly an aces cook.

"So...have you given any thought to what you're going to be doing after you graduate high school?" Seemed like Brice couldn't get through a single meal these days without someone he knew asking questions about his uncertain future. He forced a chuckle, the tasty food now forming an uncomfortable lump in his throat he had to chase down with multiple sips of tea. "Unc, I have to actually get through high school first before I can think about what comes after."

Uncle Amir spoke around a mouthful of his own food, his words slightly distorted. "You're a very smart boy. You just need to apply yourself."

Aunt Maggie clinked her spoon on the bowl and said "Alright, Amir, let the boy eat. Can't you see he's exhausted?"

Good old Aunt Maggie – always in Brice's corner. She turned to him then with questioning eyes. "How are Granny and Mom doing?"

Brice gave his usual shrug. "Yeah, you know...everybody's good."

Aunt Maggie pointed to a glossy leaflet on the table. Brice panicked for a moment, thinking it had to do with enlisting in the military until she said, "Your uncle and I are going to see the new

Egyptian exhibit at The Met tomorrow so we can drop you off at work in the morning."

He forced himself not to heave a sigh of relief. That was fantastic news. The prospect of not having to deal with an hour train ride made him ecstatic. "Sweet! If I spend any more time riding that damn subway, the MTA's gonna name a stop after me!"

Aunt Maggie laughed and rolled her eyes at his lame joke. He knew she'd get a kick out of it.

Sunday mornings at the video shop tended to be slow and Brice didn't dare complain. There was so much inventory and the like to do, it helped to have fewer customers. Multitasking was necessary, with Brice taking an order on the phone while tackling a batch of rewinds. Daisy headed out the door for her first delivery run of the day, dragging her feet. Her backpack was filled with orders, so large Brice could only see her small legs from the back.

Brice hung up as soon as he could, hoping to catch her. "Dee, wait up! I need you to swing by the Carlyle for a pickup, okay? Don't forget. The concierge is always breaking my chops because we always take too long!"

Daisy turned enough to slit her big brown eyes and put her hands on her hips. "Alright, alright. Damn, Brice. Whatchu think? I ain't got ears?"

Her cheeky New-Yorican response was typical, but that didn't make it any less humorous, and Brice responded in kind. "Daaaamn, *mamita*. Don't be giving me an attitude and shit!"

Daisy tried in vain not to laugh. She rolled her eyes, shook her head and blurted out, "You so damn corny, Brice. You been spending too much time chillin' out at the bodega!"

After Daisy left, Brice went back to the video rewind machine which played an annoying electric keyboard rendition of Beethoven's

"Fur Elise" every time a tape was inserted.

The door buzzer went off for the first time in a while and Brice looked up from his work to see Anna Miller standing in front of him.

His stomach butterflies started up instantly, but his huge smile faded in the face of her far-away stare. Something was wrong, he could feel it, but he didn't dare ask. Instead, he tried to lighten the mood. "I swear I haven't *seen Evil Dead Two* yet, so you can let down your guard!"

Anna's face moved like she was trying her best to work up a smirk, but she couldn't quite get there.

Brice's tone changed as he stepped out from behind the counter, "Hey, is everything alright? You seem upset."

Anna sighed, her shoulders slumping like they had the last time she was there. "We broke up. My boyfriend and I." She sounded so sad Brice almost felt bad that he felt like cheering. Almost.

"Can I ask what happened?"

Her voice shook as she recounted some of the specific instances that cemented her decision to bail out, gnarly stuff that made Brice want to pound the ex into a pulp. "I'm sorry you had to go through that. No one deserves that, least of all, you." He offered her his most reassuring smile. "You're better off alone rather than wasting time with someone who doesn't appreciate you."

Those emerald eyes brightened at last. "Thank you." Anna gained her composure and cleared her throat. A beat or two of silence fell between them. She didn't speak and neither did he. Okay, moment over. At least Brice had been able to help.

He was just about to walk back behind the counter when she tilted her head and looked right at him, as if she were somehow looking through him. She could probably have read every thought in his confused head.

She spoke to him clearly in her trademark smoky voice. Brice couldn't look away if he tried. "So this movie we've been talking about..."

Brice's heart stopped for a moment. He had to strain to stay calm. "Yeah, what about it?"

Anna paused for a minute. Then; "Do you want to go see it with me?"

The words might as well have been the bomb that leveled Hiroshima. Brice's body quickly went numb then hot as the world stopped turning for a split second. A warm rush of dopamine washed over him as the word "absolutely" formed on his lips. A million emotions rushed in at once. Nothing could have prepared him. What could this girl, this...woman possibly see in a seventeen-year old punk from Brooklyn?

It didn't make any sense. Maybe she just needed a safe place to park her wounded ego while she nursed her wounds and figured out her next move? Or just maybe all the goofy, boyish charm and bad jokes that rarely worked on the hardened chicks back over the Brooklyn Bridge might have actually come off as genuine swagger? Whatever the reason, Brice was on board 100%. Come what may, he planned to roll the dice and see what fate had in store for him.

"You sure you have the time?" Anna cocked an eyebrow at him, but he could tell from the twinkle in her eye that even if he didn't, Brice would have cleared his entire calendar.

He surprised even himself when he said, "I can always make time for you." It came out so smoothly, Brice was barely certain he'd even spoken it.

Giggling, Anna reached into her purse and pulled out a pen and piece of paper. She spoke as she wrote. "Here's my number. I'm going to find out what day the movie starts playing and then we'll make it official, okay?" She looked up at Brice with that grin as she handed the slip of paper, but not before asking, "Hey, wait a minute – just how old are you? I don't want to rob the cradle or anything."

Brice balked, suave manner going right out of the window. Knowing the truth would make this fortuitous event go up in flames, he gritted his teeth then lied right through them. "Yeah, I just turned twenty-one, so you're in the clear." He felt awful about it, but this was better than a winning lottery ticket as far as he was concerned.

Anna zipped up her purse, getting ready to leave. Going in for a kiss this early in the game would have been amateur hour and way too awkward. Instead, Brice held out his hand, palm up. Reaching out, Anna held it for a long second before giving him a wink and walking off.

Brice waited until she was completely out of sight before looking down. She'd written her name in flowery cursive over the magic seven digits of her phone number. He pressed it up to his nose and breathed it in. The faint scent of peaches and Sen-Sen lingered in his nostrils as he carefully folded it in two and slid it into his pocket.

Sliding another tape into the rewinder, Brice stood back and tried to absorb what just happened. He could still feel the soft warmth of her hand in his.

CHAPTER 7

With Evan and the other crew regulars off getting into some mischief they'd tell them about later, Brice and Max lounged on the front steps of Fort Brambleton High between classes, trying to soak in enough sun and fresh air to make it through the rest of the day with some sanity intact.

Max paced as Brice fiddled away on his guitar, picking at the strings with no particular tune in mind to give his restless fingers something to do while he waited for a reaction to his news.

Max stopped mid-step and turned to Brice, stroking his chin like a hardened detective in an interview. "Let me get this straight: she just walked in and asked you out?"

Brice gave him a gleeful smirk. He hadn't been able to stop grinning since it happened. "Yep!"

"And what did you say?" Max leaned down to peer into Brice's face, likely checking for the lie he was sure he'd find.

Brice calmly put down his guitar and reached out for a handshake. "Hi, I'm Brice. Have we met?" Max swatted his hand away with a scowl as Brice laughed. "What the hell do you think I said, dummy? I said 'yes'. She did ask me how old I was, though."

"And what did you tell her?" Max finally sat on the step below him, enrapt. Brice lit a cigarette, blowing a plume of spoke before he answered. "I lied through my fucking teeth and said I was 21, same as you would have done. Did you think I was gonna tell her I'm 17 and blow the whole thing?"

Max scratched his head and sat back. "Wow. That's crazy, man. You're 17 and she's *24*? That's a pretty big age difference!"

Brice agreed. He still couldn't believe it himself. "Dude, that's not even the thing I'm really worried about. I deal with the Upper East Side set all week. They're like a totally different breed. They talk different, act different, dress different. I'm afraid she's gonna figure me out quick and send me on my way!"

Max just chuckled and said, "You'll be fine, dude. Are you gonna bring her to Brooklyn and introduce her to all your friends?"

Brice fell over with laughter at such an absurd question. "Are you outta your fucking mind?"

Max cocked his head in thought, then said, "Yeah, you might want to wait a while and see how things pan out before you go and do something as risky as that!"

They parted ways a short time later to head to their respective classes. On the way, Brice noticed a glossy poster for graduation caps and gowns hanging outside the principal's office and immediately felt like he was going to be sick.

The picture-perfect teen models with their gleaming white smiles and perfect skin. Brice could bet their families weren't constantly disappointed in *them*. He had no idea what that was like. The flood gates of his self-loathing opened wide, he picked up his pace and tried to get to English class before the second bell.

Determined to make a more concerted effort to not fuck up his life any further, Brice spent the entire train ride into the city after school cramming for his upcoming English quiz. Not even the snoring bum at the end of the car could break his concentration. His nerves were frazzled as the countdown to graduation ticked away in his head.

He put on a happy face when he walked through the door of Video Star. Gil exclaimed his usual "Mr. Brice-ski" as he grabbed a handful of VHS putaways and jumped up on the ladder.

An hour later, with Daisy on deliveries and Gil taking a lunch break, Brice manned the counter alone. A pair of young gents holding tennis rackets and outfitted in crisp Izod Lacoste sportswear walked in and started perusing around. They definitely had that Ivy League look.

Brice studied the pair as they approached the counter. "Can I help you?" They could have been blueblood book ends, with one wearing a pink sports shirt and the other in the same shirt but in white. Brice had on his favorite NYU Medical sweatshirt compliments of Aunt Maggie, who worked in the university's Finance office.

The guy in pink twirled his racket as he stared at Brice's sweatshirt with curiosity that didn't appear to be genuine. He stepped back and in the snottiest, most arrogant of tones, asked, "NYU Medical? *Really*? What year are you in? My brother's a senior and my father happens to be the head of Pediatric Neurology."

A few more customers wandered in behind them, preventing Brice from doing anything but grinning and bearing the snobbery on display without comment. The guy was lucky Brice's confidence in himself was at an all-time low. On any other day, the smug prick would've been met with quite a different response.

It took effort to keep his voice low and even, but he opted for the truth. "I don't actually go there. My aunt works in the Finance office and she got me the shirt."

The guy in pink turned to his buddy and laughed. "Oh, the *Finance* office. That's greeeat. Yeah, you know...I thought we might have some mutual acquaintances. But I guess not."

Brice's hands began to tremble. At his breaking point, he prayed silently for Gil to walk in so Brice could just leave.

Mr. Pink seemed to enjoy making sport of him at this point. "So, what new releases are *really* good?

Brice shrugged, barely containing his temper. "The new release boxes are all over on that shelve over there." He pointed but the guy didn't even look. His counterpart had started to become quite fidgety and red in the face, constantly glancing at the door for an escape, but Pink Shirt didn't let up.

"Yeah. I can see that. But I want *you* to tell me what's good. My family pays a lot of money to be in this video rental club and I would like a little customer service".

Fuck this guy. Brice clenched his fist tightly enough to crack his knuckles behind the counter, ready to put his antagonist into a coma.

The two were staring each other down when Gil breezed through the door, breaking the heated tension between them. The man in white pulled his friend aside by the sleeve and said so low Brice could barely hear, "C'mon, Graham, let's just go look in the action section."

As they retreated from the counter, Brice told Gil he'd be back in ten and stalked out of the front door to the street. Tears of rage rolled down his face as he stood on the corner, his face to the sky in a pitiful effort to hide them from passersby. But none of them would have cared, anyway.

He pulled out a cigarette from his pack. Why were things so going to shit? He reached into his pocket looking for his lighter and felt a piece of paper. He pulled it out and realized it was the phone number Anna had given him.

Wow, he'd already forgotten the best thing in his life had already happened. He took a deep breath and started to feel a little better. He stared at the number, forcing his brain to remember it. Tonight was the night to call her.

When he got back to the store, the pair had gone, much to Brice's relief. Gil looked at him and said, "That guy you were waiting on was a real asshole." Brice laughed and slapped Gil on the back.

****

The clock on his bedroom wall read half past eight as Brice tried to finish up his math homework. The crumbled sliver of paper with Anna's number on it lay next to the phone. It was the moment of truth.

Setting his homework aside, he dialed the seven magic digits with shaking fingers, then grabbed his guitar as he waited for Anna to pick up so he had something to hold on to should the call not go his way.

A neon sign that read "Play it cool!" flashed in his head with each unanswered ring. It rang. And rang. And rang. Brice's stomach dropped to his feet. He should have known it was too good to be true. Anna knew he was a loser. She was just being nice to him that day.

He was just about to hang up when a soft voice on the other end said, "Hello?"

Brice pressed the phone more tightly to his ear. It didn't sound like the voice he remembered, the one that kept popping into his dreams...had she given him a wrong number? "Um...Anna?"

"Yes, who's this?"

"Uhh..it's Brice. From the video store."

Anna's voice brightened and Brice wanted to groan with relief. "Oh, hey! How are you?"

"I'm good. I'm not calling too late, am I?" The last thing Brice wanted to do was overstep on the first phone call.

"Not at all. It's not that late. And honestly, I'm a total night owl, anyway. Always have been."

Brice grinned. "Really? Me, too."

For the next hour and seven minutes – Brice counted every minute, wanting to enjoy it as long as possible – the two talked as if they were old friends just catching up. Brice was careful not to mention anything that would give away his age, perfectly content to let her do most of the talking and adding the occasional "Wow, really?" and "Oh, man; that's crazy" when needed.

They mostly talked about music, which was just fine with Brice. Anna had an encyclopedic knowledge of popular music and was into everything from The Ramones to Nina Hagen, Todd Rundgren and new age violinist Jean Luc Ponty. But her absolute favorite was mega pop star Prince. She gushed over The Purple One as if he were some sort of deity. She was also a huge John Waters fan. The campy, perverse exploits of his drag ingenue Devine tickled her to tears.

"So you mentioned you'd had an interview recently?" Curious, Brice circled back to something she'd said in passing at the beginning of their conversation.

"Oh! Yeah, it was for an assistant position at a center that specializes in teaching kids with Down's Syndrome."

Brice smiled at the excitement in her voice. "How'd it go?"

"Really well, I think. It was for a volunteer position, but the director told me I had enough credits from Marymount College for it to easily transition into a paid one. I can't wait."

Brice could tell. Anna had to be a hopeless empath to the core, with a propensity to taking in strays of all species. Lucky for him.

"Didn't you say you play guitar, too?"

His face heating, Brice swallowed hard. "Um...yeah."

"Could you play me something? I'd love to hear it."

The moment foretold by his school buddies was upon him, but Brice refused to chicken out. He played her few simple things he knew wouldn't sound like trash. Brice didn't know how she felt about his playing, but Anna was very polite and said he had a "cool, raw style" – a sweet way of saying he needed to practice more. It didn't sting as much as Brice thought it would, coming from her. As the daughter of showbiz folks who put a high premium on musicality, she'd told him they'd forced her to take piano lessons from the age of five. Anna was likely a world class player herself but downplayed it, probably because she felt there was no way she could match her father's creative achievements. Everyone had something they struggled with.

As the conversation wound down, Anna segued to the business of their pending first date. "So, the movie definitely opens this weekend, but they haven't posted a schedule yet. Why don't we connect in a day or two? We can pick a time and you know, make it official."

Brice, now glowing on the inside and figuring they should end the conversation on a high note, said, "Uh, okay, yeah, absolutely. So...I guess we'll catch up later?"

Anna agreed and wished him good night. He hung up the phone and stared up at the ceiling. That had actually gone well! Perfect, even! His heart raced with excitement. The timing couldn't be any worse though, given all his issues with school, but an opportunity like this with a girl – a woman – like Anna only came along once in a lifetime. He could either play it safe or get up on the high wire and risk a real catastrophe. In his heart of hearts, he knew she was a risk worth taking.

With another grueling school day behind him, Brice and the crew took the scenic route home. Third Avenue was a hotbed of activity at three in the afternoon. Legions of smoking hot Catholic high school chicks waited for connecting buses as he and the boys put on their best tough guy acts, looking for any willing participants in their poorly choreographed ruse. No one paid them any mind today, and as they got back to the neighborhood, Brice caught a glimpse of someone by the supermarket that caught his attention. He said goodbye to the guys and crossed the street to a little old lady in a tiger-print coat struggling with a paper bag full of groceries.

He walked up beside her and in his best Jimmy Cagney voice said, "Now listen lady, we saw you stuffing that box of prunes into your girdle. You almost got away with it, too. Don't make any trouble and we might go easy on you."

She almost jumped out of her skin, then spun around and seeing it was her grandson giving her a hard time, gave a happy squeal with her hand on her cheek. "My baby!" She put a hand over her heart. "You little brat, you scared me half to death. I thought I forgot to pay for something. Come here!"

Brice took the surprisingly heavy bag from her and gave his grandmother a tremendous hug before they began walking towards her apartment. She thanked him for carrying her bag before she asked, "What's going on? Your mother said you're having some problems in school?"

Brice didn't want her to worry. Better someone in his life think he had it somewhat together. "You know, it's just normal teenage stuff. I'm just trying to focus on getting my life in order. There always seems to be stuff going on, a never-ending sea of distractions. I'm so sick of stressing over everything".

She stopped to grab his hand and said, "Listen honey, everything is going to work out. Just say a prayer that God gives you the strength to overcome your obstacles."

Brice laughed hard at that. "Why can't *you* just say the prayer for me? I haven't been to mass in years. God might not recognize me. You've got way more pull than I do!"

His grandmother let out a belly laugh right there on the street. "Are you kidding me? I pray for you every day. And I light a candle, too...so that God keeps you safe."

"Awwww...who do I love?" Heart full to bursting, Brice gave her a big kiss on her forehead.

As they approached her building, she grabbed the bag of groceries from him. "Okay honey, I've got it from here".

"Are you sure?" Brice raised an eyebrow at the multiple steps she'd have to climb to get inside.

She just laughed. "Yes, yes. Whaddya think? Your grandmother's a weakling? We spent three weeks at sea on that miserable boat when we came over from Europe. Nothing but macaroni. Breakfast, lunch and dinner! You think a shopping bag is gonna be a problem?"

She had a point. Brice gave her a final hug and kiss and headed home. Brice was just about to head upstairs to knock out his math homework when had a got the sneaking suspicion Max and Evan might be up to no good. He wanted in, so he did an about-face and marched over to HQ instead. Homework could wait a while.

CHAPTER 8

Mrs. Valetta, the neighborhood fluff-and-fold matron, stood across the street near the laundromat sucking on a Virginia Slim as Brice stood outside HQ waiting for Max to let him in. When he smiled at her and waved, she only gave him a disapproving scowl. Brice just shrugged to himself. She was probably one of the neighbors who usually called the police on their parties.

To his surprise, Grant opened the door with his three-year-old daughter in his arms. Grant and his first real girlfriend Noreen had tied the knot when they were both nineteen upon discovering she was expecting. They gave it a good two years before realizing they were just too young to make it work. Grant had too much rabbit in his blood to settle down. They made an amicable arrangement and had been doing their best to co-parent ever since.

"What's shaking there, Bricey?" Barefoot and wearing a Black Sabbath t-shirt and tattered jeans, Grant stepped back to allow Brice entrance. Brice played the usual peek-a-boo bit with the toddler as she giggled and cooed. "Man, she is getting big!" he said.

Brice found Tristan hanging out on the couch and playing his bass guitar as he strolled into the living room. Brice said "what's up, man?" and made his way upstairs to Max's bedroom. He could hear music blasting from the speakers before he burst through the door.

Preoccupied with rolling joints, Max and Evan nearly hit the ceiling at the sudden intrusion. They both breathed a heavy sigh of relief at the sight of Brice.

Still hyperventilating, Max said, "Dude, I thought it was my old man. I would have been up the fucking creek if he saw me rolling up a doob. Ever since he caught a couple minutes of that after-school special where the kid smokes some angel dust and nosedives off a roof because he thought he could fly, he's been on this 'just say No' kick."

Evan popped a fresh joint into his mouth and started laughing. "Bro, I loved that fucking movie!" he said as he reached for a pack of matches on the bed.

Brice snatched it from his hand. "You're not lighting that thing up here."

Evan's face twisted in confusion. "Why the hell not?"

"Hello, dumbass – Max's niece is downstairs. She's gonna catch a contact high while she's playing with her dolls." Brice had limits to his wayward behavior when little kids were involved. Rolling his eyes at his friend, Brice peeked out the window at the sunny day outside those walls. Picture perfect.

An idea popped into his head. He looked back at Max and Evan and waggled his thick eyebrows. "You two clowns up for a little 'mesh cloud' action?" The two boys cracked wide, mischievous grins and responded in unison: "Absolutely!"

Armed with enough herb to put an elephant into a coma, they all grabbed their jackets and headed for the park.

The overhead fence screens that covered the park's baseball diamonds made a perfect observation deck to the Narrows and neighboring borough. A lush panoramic view of Staten Island was the perfect backdrop for a late afternoon of getting high as a kite and laughing until they felt sick. Once completely baked, one got the sensation of floating on a "mesh cloud".

The trio found an empty diamond and started their ascent. Getting to the top was easy. With a childhood spent running wild in the streets, every kid in the neighborhood had a PhD in fence and garage climbing. Getting down in such an impaired state was always the tricky part. Brice stepped to the side and motioned for Evan to lead the way. "Ladies first." He sniggered as Evan pulled up his pants and started to climb. Max and Brice followed.

A warm breeze rustled the trees as the tug boats and cargo ships glided along the Narrows. Each found their favorite spots and hunkered down. Evan lay back on the rusty wire and said, "Oh man, I so need this right now."

Max lit up the first joint and took a big hit. He passed it clockwise to Brice "Did you call that chick yet?"

Evan lifted his head to look at them both. "Who, Lindsey's friend?"

Max, still recovering from a coughing fit, shook his head. "Nah, man. It's some twenty-four-year-old chick that comes into the video store. She totally asked this guy out."

Brice had a difficult time hiding his smug smile. He finished taking a long drag and passed to Evan, who stared at him in wonder. "*Twenty-Four*?! Damn! And she lives in Manhattan?"

Still holding the burning smoke in his lungs, Brice simply nodded.

Evan looked at Brice sideways. "So did you 'seal the deal'?"

Brice let out the smoke with a deep cough and laughed. "Dude, are you not listening? I just met her. We only talked once. I gotta at least take her out on one date before we do that."

Evan, now with slits for eyes, giggled and said, "Sorry, man I'm really fucking high right now."

Max was suffering from a critical case of smile-itis and blurted out, "Me, too!"

Evan tried to be serious, making an effort to force his eyes to focus on Brice's face. "Where you gonna take her?"

Brice passed the joint back to Max. "The city, I guess. She wants to see *Evil Dead Two*." Nothing about that could even make him nervous right now. He might as well be floating into the trees.

Evan stretched out and folded his arms behind his head. "Check out Brice, moving up in the world."

Completely baked now, Brice looked out over the water that sparkled like diamonds and managed to say, "I don't know about all that. It'd probably be ten times easier to just hook up with one of Lindsey's friends. At least I know how to deal with that situation. This is a whole different kinda horse race."

A long pause stretched on as the friends rested their heavy eyelids and listened to the wind. Evan, having evidently reached the perfect state of bliss, jumped up with fist in the air out of nowhere. "Anyway...long live the Brotherhood of the Mesh Cloud!"

They spent the next full hour laughing, zoning out and bullshitting about this and that. The sun had just begun to set when the three amigos did their best to climb down off their cloud without breaking anything. They all stumbled back home sleepy and content after an afternoon of male bonding enhanced by THC.

Brice took a quick nap before dinner and was getting back to the books when the phone rang.

"Hello?"

"Hey, you busy?" Anna's voice on the other end of the line sounded like angels singing.

Brice's heart did the fluttering thing, but he managed to keep it cool. "Not at all...what's up?"

He could hear her rifling through the pages of a newspaper. "Okay, so *Evil Dead Two* is playing at Loew's Orpheum on Saturday at 8:30. Does that work for you?"

Did it work for him? That was like her asking him if he'd mind winning the lottery. "Cool! Sounds great." He'd have to get Jordan to cover the last few hours of his shift to make it work, but Brice wasn't going to let such a minor detail get in the way of destiny.

They chatted for a bit and were just about to end the call when Anna paused for a second and said, "So...there's one more thing. Other than Saturday night, are you busy doing anything else this weekend?"

His heart thumped even harder than it did when he first picked up the phone. Brice took a few seconds to calm himself enough to think straight. "I work on Saturday until about six, but other than that, I think I'm free. Why?"

"Well, Friday night I have to go to this function with my mother, but she and her boyfriend Mel are driving out to the Hamptons right afterwards. I've got the house to myself all weekend. Do you wanna maybe...stay overnight here with me?"

Brice didn't even notice how long they fell quiet while Anna's question lingered in the air. The thought of a pre-first date sleepover left him anesthetized with joy. Something like a supernova burst through him at the mere thought of it.

"You know," Anna said, voice sultry and tempting enough in his ear to make the decision for him, "if you've got work in the morning, you'd be right here and then we could go to the movies after you're done."

Brice's excitement nearly made him throw the phone receiver across the room, cord and all, but no – he remembered his mantra just in time: Just play it cool. "Sure. That would be great, but didn't you just say you have that function to go to?"

Anna paused to clear her throat. "I do, but you could just hang out here at the house until I'm back. It's only a few hours."

That made all the sense in the world to Brice. He paced, unable to keep still. "I mean, if you're okay with me hanging out in the house alone with you not being there..."

"I'm totally cool with it," Anna said with a note of finality. "Then it's settled –that's the plan. Okay, just one last thing and I promise I'll let you go. I have a quick dentist appointment Friday afternoon. Do you just want to meet me there and then we can head back to my house together?"

At this point, Anna could have asked Brice to help her rob a bank and he would've agreed. "Sure! Whatever you want to do is fine with me. You got the address of the dentist's office?" They wrapped up the details of their next meeting and finally said good night. After he hung up, Brice glanced at the address he'd jotted down in his notebook. He hadn't seen this plot twist coming and needed to start working out the details in his head.

Brice threw open his bedroom window for some fresh air before lighting up a cigarette. He climbed out onto the fire escape and blew big rings of smoke into the air. The half moon looked like a big bright crooked smile as the clouds blew past it. He hoped Jordan would sport something similar when Brice swung by his house at some point during the week. The level of a favor Brice needed would require an appearance in person.

****

The sound of Max chuckling at Brice's expense reached Brice as he writhed in misery at his desk. English class was particularly unbearable today, the odor of the cafeteria's pungent lunch special wafting in through the open windows.

Brice glanced up at the yellowing white clock on the wall. It hadn't moved an inch since the last time he looked, and he could have sworn that was some time ago.

Ms. DeLucca was quite a sight. Standing there at a mere four feet nine on the nose, the English teacher was a mini Mussolini if ever there was one; at least two hundred pounds, huge glasses with thick black frames and a personality that made all her students want to run for cover.

She held her textbook high in the air and in her best fake English accent started, "'O, that this too-too solid flesh would melt, thaw, and resolve itself into a dew! Or that the everlasting had not fix'd his canon 'gainst self-slaughter!'"

She put the book down after reading the complete soliloquy and scanned the faces of her students. "Pretty heavy stuff, huh? What do you think Hamlet has on his mind?" The last thing she said floated somewhere near the front of Brice's mind unheard as he turned toward the window. What was Anna doing right now?

"Mr. Laine!" Ms. DeLucca slapped a palm flat on his desk so hard, he nearly jumped out of his skin. She slit her beady eyes at him. "You seem to be deep in thought over Hamlet's predicament. What would be your assessment of this line?"

Brice's face practically caught fire, it suddenly felt so hot. He sat up and cleared his throat. "I'm sorry. What was the question?" His classmates collectively chuckled and the tips of Brice's ears caught fire, too.

"*Hamlet*, Mr. Laine. First soliloquy. Act one."

Thank God...Brice had perused that passage earlier in the week and gave what he hoped was an acceptable, if not disjointed, answer. He didn't have to wait to see if Mussolini found it acceptable as well; the fifth period bell initiated a Pavlovian response from his antsy classmates racing for the door, saving Brice from further agony.

Brice was halfway down the hall when Max called out for him to wait up, panting when he reached him. "Hey, what's up?"

Brice collapsed backward against the lockers, angry with himself for the urge to cry that suddenly strangled him. "That fat little witch is so gonna fail my ass. I can taste it."

A frown creased Max's forehead. "You really think so? You snapped back a pretty legit explanation on that Hamlet question."

"Yeah, well...I dunno." Brice shrugged, swallowing again and again. He had to keep it together. No way could he break down like a wuss in front of his buddy. "She already told my mother unless I get my shit together and fast, I'm going down like the fucking Titanic." Squaring his shoulders, Brice tried to brush it all off and clapped a hand on Max's back. "Anyway, what's on your docket for the weekend?" Brice didn't want to think about his problems any longer than necessary.

Max rubbed his mitts together and pursed his lips. "The Cherry Bombs are playing Friday at LeRoxx. You in?"

Brice pinched Max on the cheek and said, "Sorry, Charlie. I'm gonna be busy winning over the affections of a certain someone way over on the Isle of Mana-hatta."

Max looked thoroughly confused. "You said that was going down on Saturday", he said, making Brice laugh. So much had changed since then. Brice whispered in his ear. "Oh, I forgot to tell you. It's since developed into a – wait for it...a full-on 'sleepover weekend'"

Max pushed him back into the lockers in shock. "Get the fuck outta here! Are you serious? Man, I'm really starting to like this chick and I've never even met her!" As the two started walking toward the cafeteria, Brice said, "I swear I couldn't make this shit up if I tried." They both did their best not to gag once they met up with the crew who were already hunkered down at the lunch room table staring down at full trays of prison-grade mystery slop.

Jordan and his family had a nice house a few blocks away from Lindsey's place, which Gil was able to buy back in the day when he had his own garment factory. The subject of Brice's visit looked suspicious when he let Brice inside. Smirking, Brice popped into the cozy kitchen, where Jordan's mom was humming along to some Italian song playing on the radio.

"Hey, Moms," Brice said, giving her a one-armed hug.

"Oh – hi, Brice! You stayin' for dinner?"

It broke Brice's heart to say no – she was a badass on the skillet, after all – but he had a mountain of homework waiting for him at home. And her son to convince to help Brice with his cause.

Back in the hallway, Jordan folded his arms and narrowed his eyes. "So what's so important that we had to discuss it in person?"

Brice grabbed Jordan by the arm and led him into the living room to talk. Jordan broke free as soon as they were out of earshot. "Well?"

Taking a breath, Brice started to reveal his plan. "First you gotta promise me you won't say no."

Jordan almost fell over onto the nearby couch laughing. "Uh, nice try," he said once he'd recovered, "but I've got to know what I'm agreeing to first."

Brice studied a loose thread in the carpet at his feet. "You know that girl from the store, Anna Miller?"

"Yeah, that rich chick with the asshole boyfriend. What about her?"

All Brice's rehearsed lines went out the window. How could he sell this? In his desperation, he just blurted out the first thing that came to mind. "She asked me out on a date and I need you to cover half my shift this Saturday. *You cannot say no.*"

Jordan's mouth fell open. "Hold on. You expect me to believe that she asked *you* out? Bullshit. There's no way. What about the boyfriend?"

Brice shrugged. "I guess she got sick of his shit, so they broke up. We'd been talking about *Evil Dead Two* coming out, then one day she wandered into the store and just asked me if I wanted to go with her."

Jordan stepped back and rubbed his chin before he smiled. "You're a lucky fucking bastard!"

Brice winced. "Oh, and there's more."

"What do you mean there's more?" Jordan's brow furrowed, making Brice take a deep breath.

"She wants me to sleep over her house the night before we go."

"See, now I know you're fucking lying." Jordan said, chuckling so hard his stomach hurt "You pushed your little ruse too far and yeah...you're full of shit!"

Brice realized how absurd this must've sounded to his buddy. He exhaled, looked Jordan square in the eye and said, "I swear on my grandmother's life I'm telling you the truth."

Jordan sobered. "Awww man, this is my only Saturday off this month." But he now had his proof. He stepped back, studying Brice. He was quiet so long Brice started to worry but Jordan said, "Fine, but it's gonna cost you big – really big!"

Brice's knees trembled with relief, but the wicked look on Jordan's face just then gave him pause. "You know how big?"

Brice shrugged, almost afraid to know.

Raising his chin, Jordan said, "You're getting me a date with

Lindsey."

Brice couldn't help it and burst out laughing. "Are you fucking nuts? How many times are we gonna go over this?"

"Okay!" Jordan held up his hands in surrender. "But you at least have to tell her that I bought a guitar and I'm getting really friggin' good! Deal?"

Brice sighed. He couldn't see any harm and agreed, but not without adding,

"You're a sick puppy, bro...but yeah, I'll slip in a little white lie if it'll make you feel better."

On his way back to his mother's place, Brice figured his grandmother really had been praying for him when he spotted Lindsey sitting on her stoop and talking on the phone. She waved him over. As soon as she ended her call, she started giggling.

Brice grinned at her. "What?"

In her best bratty kid voice she started singing. "Bricey's got a girlfriend..."

God, news traveled fast in this neighborhood. He rolled his eyes. "Yeah, yeah...take it easy. We haven't even gone on a date yet."

Lindsey, now touching up her nails with the brightest fire engine red known to man said, "Oh, stop. I'm sure she's gonna fall head over heels!"

Brice started to ask how she'd heard about his new relationship, but Lindsey's mom called her in for dinner. He leaned down and gave her a goodbye peck on the cheek. "Oh, did you hear Jordan started playing guitar?"

Lindsey gave him a skeptical stare. Brice made sure to keep his promise and added, "Apparently, he's getting really good."

She just chuckled and closed the screen door behind her. Brice, having honored his end of his deal with Jordan, walked home with a new pep in his step.

Later that evening, Brice was helping to clear the dinner table when Aunt Maggie asked about his plans for the coming weekend. It pained him to lie to her, but he needed to create a situation where no one would notice he'd be off the grid all weekend.

He dropped his plate into the standing dishwater in the sink and said carefully, "Well, I don't know...Friday I'm going out and then I have to work Saturday and then yeah, it's all up in the air. I'll probably crash at Mom's or Granny's."

Apparently pleased with his answer, his aunt smiled and headed out of the kitchen. "We're around all weekend, so just let us know."

Once the dishes were done, Brice dashed upstairs to his room and called Jordan. Though still none too pleased about having to cover his Saturday shift, he confirmed he was still on board with the plan. After telling him that he'd made Lindsey aware of his newfound guitar prowess, Jordan cackled diabolically and said, "It won't be long now!"

Brice just shook his head and told him to keep dreaming.

****

According to reports Brice had been hearing from his coworkers, actor Robin Williams was in town doing press for his movie *Good Morning, Vietnam* and was now making sporadic evening appearances at Video Star. During the process, Williams had taken up temporary residence across the street from the store in a plush, newly constructed high-rise with his former babysitter turned expecting wife.

Over the years, Brice had become all but immune to daily interactions with the vast array of entertainment heavyweights that walked through the door. Mary Tyler Moore herself had once yelled at him in front of a store full of customers for accidentally giving away her reserved copy of *Out of Africa*. When it came to dealing with "stars", it was safe to say he was way past gushing.

On a quiet afternoon with just he and Gil manning the counter, Brice had his nose in his English textbook and was busy deciphering a tricky line from *Hamlet* when the phone rang.

Brice picked it up. "Video."

There was a pause before a very calm voice on the other end of the phone said, "This is Robin Williams. I've got a video stuck in my VCR; do you think you could send someone up?"

A chill ran down Brice's spine at the prospect of some serious one-on-one time with the comedy legend. As he quickly closed his textbook, Brice's mind was slung back in time to Mrs. Venturini's fourth grade class, exactly one day after the television premier of *Mork and Mindy*. Every kid in class was floored by the quirky sitcom and couldn't stop saying "Shazzbot" or "Na-Noo-Na-Noo". It was an extremely significant cultural phenomenon for a room full of eleven-year-olds.

So much for not gushing! Brice composed himself and said, "That shouldn't be a problem, sir. We'll have someone up shortly."

After hanging up, Brice told Gil he'd be back in twenty. He then grabbed a small screwdriver set and flew out the door with the animated stride of an elderly couple in matching sweat suits doing a power walk through Central Park.

Brice was standing in the lobby in under eight minutes. The doorman gave him a reassuring nod, letting him know he'd gotten "the call" and received the necessary clearances to allow Brice to proceed.

Within seconds Brice rocketed toward the heavens in a finely crafted elevator, minutes away from a completely unexpected private meeting with a favorite celebrity. The thirty-story ride gave him plenty of time to imagine a host of possible dialogue:

"Gee Brice, what's a funny, good-looking young guy like you doing working at a video rental store?"

"I think I might have a part for you in my next film..."

"That's the funniest thing I ever heard, B-Man – did you ever think about writing comedy?"

"Brice, do you know what a personal assistant does?"

Running simultaneously in his head was a collage of every movie, bit, character, and voice he'd ever heard Robin do. Brice didn't want to be caught off guard if Robin made a reference to one of his lesser-known works during the chat.

Now at the penthouse suite, Brice rang the doorbell with fingers trembling with nervous anticipation and waited for what felt like an eternity. There was only one door on the entire floor. This was no *pied a terre*.

Then the tall door opened, and there he stood...a short, tired-looking individual that vaguely resembled the great Robin Williams, in a wrinkled t-shirt and shorts, who said in almost a whisper, "Thanks for coming up." In a split second, the grandeur that Brice had envisioned turned into an extremely unglamorous event. The man led Brice through a series of tastefully furnished rooms to the scene of the crime. The VCR had been carefully extracted from its entertainment center home and placed on the floor for Brice – "The Expert" – to perform the required surgery.

There Brice stood, still expecting a rip-roaring, knee-slapping verbal roller coaster ride with the kooky Russian defector from

Moscow on the Hudson or even the mad-libbing coke fueled stand-up comedian he'd seen on HBO. Instead, the only sounds in the room were of Mr. Williams doing an Academy Award-winning impersonation of a wall, and of Brice blasting sighs of exasperation from his nostrils as he tried to extract a very worn out video cassette and its tangled viscera from an extremely uncooperative machine. Upon further examination and discovery that the video cassette didn't even belong to Video Star, Brice very politely conveyed to Mr. Williams, that regarding the level of technical proficiency needed to remedy the problem, Brice was simply out of his league.

Brice then performed the painstaking task of stuffing the video with its tentacle-like entrails back into its rectangular plastic home, then reattaching the black metallic VCR shell without making it look worse than it did when he'd originally found it. Upon completion, Brice and Mr. Williams proceeded to the exit for the inevitable departure from his private and shockingly subdued world. In New York City, it was quite customary for individuals in any service-related industry to earn a tip for even remotely satisfactory performance. In Brice's book, the visit definitely qualified as outstanding, even with the unresolved outcome.

But Mr. Williams opened the door, gave Brice the obligatory "Thaaanks" accompanied by the most painful attempt at a smile he'd ever seen, and sent Brice on his way. Empty handed.

As he headed for the elevator, Brice thought to himself, "Damn Sam, did Robin Williams just totally stiff me on the tip?" The answer was a resounding yes.

The elevator ride down was a lot less exciting than the one going up. Brice was politely escorted by security out through the service exit and onto the side street. He dipped into a nearby pizzeria and bought himself a slice and soda for a job well done. "Screw that guy," he muttered to himself between bites.

Back at the store, Brice told Gil his tale and from that point forward, the general consensus among he and his coworkers was that Robin Williams was a total knob. As Brice got back to *Hamlet*, he found himself chuckling despite the disappointing afternoon. It actually was kind of cool having a part time gig where getting chewed out by the likes of Mary Tyler Moore and being pissed off at Robin Williams was all in a day's work.

CHAPTER 9

Friday arrived sooner than Brice expected, leaving him a ball of nervous energy all morning.

He, Max, Evan and the rest of the third period gym class hooligans stood on the basketball courts in tube socks and shorts, pretending to care about the day's assignment. Mr. Fried's whistle blew every few seconds as a series of half court pickup games commenced.

After yet another unsuccessful attempt at a three-point jumper, Max turned to Brice and nudged him in the ribs. "So tonight's the night, huh?"

Brice tried his best to cover Evan on defense but failed miserably with his mind in two different places. "Yeah bud-dy!"

Evan snorted and gave Brice a patronizing look. "Hey Brice, do you and I need to have, you know...'the talk'?"

Brice gave a hearty laugh and dodged the basketball coming straight for his head. "Nah, man. I was with your mom last night. She covered just about everything I need to know."

Max laughed so hard at that he held his stomach and fell backwards onto the ball court. Evan grabbed a rebound from the air and passed it to another player before he said, "Hey Brice, you got any naked pictures of your mother?"

"No. Why?"

Evan had a big, goofy smile. "You wanna buy some?"

Max and Brice hit the floor laughing again as Evan, now fancying himself the comeback king, walked over to the water fountains for a victory sip.

Later on, as Brice changed in the locker room, Max came over to talk. Dragging a comb through his silky locks, he turned and said, "Seriously dude, when a twenty-four-year-old chick invites you to crash at her place for the weekend, it's like a given that you're gonna bang, right?"

Brice shook his head. Of course the thought – many thoughts – like that had crossed his mind. "Yeah, I guess so. But I don't wanna go in there like I'm expecting it to happen. She'll deal me a hand and I'll play it."

Evan walked over just then and jumped right into their conversation. "Brice is gonna play the hand cool. 'Cool Hand Brice'."

As they all laughed again and walked towards class, Max turned to Evan and said, "Dude, you gotta stop with these lame ass fucking sayings."

The three o'clock bell rang out as Brice bolted from class and towards Mom's place to get ready. It was "go time".

The plan needed to be executed with precision. With no time to waste, he skipped the usual long walk home with the crew for a nearby shuttle bus that let him off right by his mother's apartment.

No sense taking a chance waiting for the elevators down in the lobby. The possibility of some unsolicited chit chat from anyone of the building's dozen or so elderly residents could set him back and fuck up the whole thing. Brice felt like rocket fuel pulsed through his veins as he leapt up the building stairwell two steps at a time to the third-floor apartment. He needed to be showered, shaved and on a Manhattan-bound express in a half hour, tops. His duffle bag was carefully stowed away in his bottom drawer, ready to go.

Brice carefully slid the key in the lock of the paint-chipped door.

Echoes of voices from above and below bellowed through hallways as he tried to be as quiet as humanly possible to avoid detection. The deadbolt turned over without a sound. Brice slipped through the doorway, careful not to make any loud noises in the hallway.

"Ma?" Cringing at the volume of his own voice, Brice waited like a statue for a reply. No answer. He swiftly shut the door behind him and dashed though the darkened main hall towards the shower. Scalding hot water cascaded over his body as he scrubbed from head to toe with the fervor of a surgeon late for a quadruple bypass.

Freshly scrubbed and wrapped in a towel, Brice wiped away the mist from the medicine cabinet mirror to take a peek at his mug. He meticulously checked his face for any zits or blackheads that may have appeared since his last inspection. His mouth fell open when he noticed a whitehead protruding from his left temple. With a firm squeeze between his forefinger and thumb, he struck the new offender from the record.

Brice leaned on a side wall and took a deep breath to ground himself against the constant tingling and dizziness. Excitement at this level was typically reserved for weekends on Seducer's Charm's road crew with the prospect of post-show fun at HQ. He continued with his grooming ritual, applying some hair gel, deodorant and a healthy dose of fragrant after shave for good measure.

Now, ready with his trusty duffel bag slung over his shoulder and smelling as fresh as a daisy, Brice walked into the kitchen. Mom's ashtray and fresh pack of smokes lay there on the table. He placed his note just underneath it: "Hey Ma, gotta work this weekend. Probably staying at Aunt Maggie's. See you Sunday. Love, Brice." And with that, he slipped out the door to catch a train into the city.

Friday afternoons on the avenue were always bustling, especially when the weather was nice. Brice knew he'd run into at least a half dozen friends or acquaintances between his apartment and the train station. He made a conscious effort to stay off the main thoroughfare, keeping his head down and striding briskly along the

75

alternate route. Just as he feared, Brice rounded the corner and had to avert his eyes from an old school chum who would certainly be intent on catching up.

Brice proceeded down the station's crumbling steps and into the cool subterranean underworld to catch his ride. The sound of an oncoming Manhattan bound express increased in intensity with every passing second. He fumbled through his pockets looking for the magic coin that would gain him entry.

As he slipped the bronzed token into the slot, he pushed his full weight into the turnstile and slid through. He jettisoned himself and his duffle bag down the steps, making it into the idling subway car without a second to spare. The warning "stand clear of the closing doors" bellowed from the speakers above Brice's head as the motorman put the iron and steel freight into gear.

Brice found a free seat by the window and put his feet on the edge of the adjacent bench. Flashbacks of early childhood trips into the city with Granny brought a smile to his face.

He stretched and made himself more comfortable. By a stroke of luck Brice happened to pick a car whose newly serviced air conditioning system insured he wouldn't exit onto the street looking and smelling like a sweaty pig. He caught a glimpse of his reflection in the scratched window. A few subtle dabs of Mom's makeup foundation did the trick for keeping his blemishes in check. The light scruff on his chin would hopefully add on a year or two and dismiss any suspicions of his not being of a certain age; he remembered that bit of advice given to him by the Seducer himself, whose charm and charisma had yielded more than a bedpost's worth of notches.

Brice closed his eyes and tried to relax as legions of private grammar school kids in pleats and blue plaid chattered like magpies. He chuckled to himself hearing the subjects of their banter: secret crushes, gossip and the general naïve musings of thirteen-year-olds who hadn't a clue about what was heading their way, all spoken with the seriousness of dignitaries discussing lofty geopolitical matters.

All that seemed like a lifetime ago for Brice.

The sun shone brightly as the hulking behemoth emerged from its pathway underground and onto the rails of the Manhattan Bridge. Beams of buttery sunlight blasted through the windows and illuminated every inch of the car. It felt...symbolic somehow. Like this chance with Anna had shot light through the darkness of his life. Maybe that was a bit dramatic, but that's how Brice felt as he watched the city fly by.

The rhythmic pulse of steel wheels on iron tracks put Brice into a trance like state as he stared out over the waterfront. The view this time of day was picturesque to say the least. The World Trade Center, South Street Seaport and downtown skyline were all in full view, accented by the afternoon sunlight dancing off the East River currents below.

When the train finally pulled to a stop a bit later, Brice hopped off and plodded his way along the platform with the rest of the restless New Yorkers. The 86th Street exit sign came into view. Brice walked by two sewer rats engaged in an intense tug of war over a pizza crust and glanced at the large clock overhead. He was making good time.

Brice exited through the carousel, up the stairs and onto Lexington Avenue. Squinting at the sudden onslaught of sunlight, Brice spun to get his bearings. Right – there was the intersection he needed to get to. As he cracked his knuckles and lit up a smoke for the four-block walk, Brice found himself caught between an endless sea of working-class stiffs looking to get off the island and back to their middle class enclaves and a smaller segment of the neighborhood's gentry looking to get out to their million dollar coastal hideaways for sunset.

He passed a quaint flower shop on the corner and looked in the window. The floral displays dazzled but the prices definitely put them out of Brice's reach. The owner, a shapely middle-aged woman in a sharp suit, was scrambling around the store frenetically, likely trying to wrap things up for the day. She spotted Brice ogling her wares and walked outside.

"Anything catch your eye?" Her painted lips smirked as she raised an eyebrow at her own double entendre.

Brice smirked back at her. She must have been a real man eater back in her day. He flicked his cigarette butt into the street. "They're all beautiful, but a little too rich for my blood."

"What's the occasion?"

Brice couldn't help it and blushed like a little boy. "A first date."

A wicked, playful smile washed over the woman's face as she rubbed her hands together. "Wait right here!"

"Um, alright." Brice scratched his chin and stood there awkwardly in front of the shop. Within a minute, she bolted back out the door with a large bouquet of multicolored roses wrapped in a large sheath of glossy patterned florist's paper.

Brice blinked at the display. "What's this?"

The woman beamed. "Well, somebody ordered this batch of beauties for pick up at three. They obviously forgot to come and get them, so my loss is your gain. I'm trying to get out of dodge in five minutes, so needless to say, they are available for sale."

He needed to go to church with his grandmother at the first opportunity; her prayers were working overtime. "How much?"

She tapped her cheek in thought for a second, then said, "Well, given the circumstances, and the fact that you're so damn cute, 20 bucks should cover it."

That was a deal he could not pass up. "Sold!" He reached into his jeans' pocket and pulled out a crumpled up 20 dollar bill. She slid it off his palm as she handed him the bouquet.

"Now go make an epic first impression!" The woman reached up and pulled down the store front riot gate then blew him a kiss.

Brice marveled at the vibrant bushel and breathed in the fragrant buds. They didn't look real. Mother nature really had her shit together. He thanked the woman and proceeded on his way with a little extra spring in his step.

CHAPTER 10

As he rounded the corner to his final destination, Brice eyed a parked Buick right outside of the towering office building and sat down on its already dented hood. He did his best to hide the enormous bouquet behind his duffle bag. A steady procession of older folks in well-made clothes ambled by arm in arm as he waited patiently for Anna to appear. They were supposed to meet up ten minutes ago. What if he had written down the wrong address?

What if she'd changed her mind?

Brice was just about to ask a passerby for the time when the doors to the high rise opened and Anna stepped outside, making Brice's breath catch in his throat and choke him.

As she approached, Brice jumped off the car and swung the colossal bouquet from behind his back and handed them to her. "These are for you."

A huge smile erupted on her face. "Oh my God, they are absolutely beautiful! That is so sweet of you! And I am so sorry I'm late; they had to take in an emergency root canal and bumped my appointment back fifteen minutes." She finally took a breath. "Have you been waiting out here long"?

Brice shook his head. "Nah, not really." His words came out in a murmur since he could barely keep track of what he was saying for taking her in. Anna was absolutely radiant. Playing it cool proved much harder than it seemed. He wanted to swoop her slender frame up into his arms and profess his unwavering commitment to her for all eternity. Instead, he leaned in and gave her a quick peck on the cheek and said "You really look great. Did you get your hair cut?"

Anna grinned and her eyes lit up all over again. At least Brice was doing something right so far. "Wow, good eye! It was so overdue. I got it colored, too. Do you like it? Feel it – it's like silk."

Anna stared up at him as he gingerly reached out and touched her hair. It really did feel like silk as the locks flowed through his fingers. Not wanting to be too forward, Brice let his hand drop.

Anna looked around at the traffic with a hand on her hip. "You know what, this corner's always impossible to get a cab. You wanna walk over to 84th Street and give it a try?" Brice was so smitten, he would have agreed to pulling her all the way home in a rickshaw if she'd wanted. He nodded, still barely able to speak in the face of her loveliness.

Anna placed her nose just above her bouquet and breathed them in. Her eyes rolled back with delight. She looked up at him through her long, long lashes and Brice's heart began to thump in his throat instead of his chest. Her voice very soft, she said, "Do you want to hold my hand?"

Brice wasn't sure how much longer he could keep playing it cool with this kind of talk going on. He hadn't anticipated getting overwhelmed with these kinds of feelings and longed for some kind of playbook to give him a little more direction on how to handle them. "Um, do you *want* me to hold your hand?"

Anna smiled in answer then stood up on her tippy toes, pulling Brice in close and kissing him hard on the mouth.

Nothing up until this point in his life had ever felt so right, especially in the romance department. The kiss, though only a few seconds long, felt like it lasted an hour. Hell, a whole lifetime.

Brice, flushed and numbed to his core, stepped back and said "I'll take that as a yes," and the two walked off hand in hand.

The traffic on 84th Street was off the charts and resembled one of those Paris roundabouts he'd seen in movies where drivers make up their own rules. Bedlam was an understatement. Brice started to feel like an idiot, unsuccessfully trying to flag down each taxi that whizzed by with a fare already in the back seat. He glanced at Anna, still marveling at and smelling the flowers instead of watching his blunders. What a good call on those.

Finally, an unoccupied cab came into view and quickly pulled over. Brice opened the door, and with duffle bag in hand, jumped into the back seat after Anna. She shouted the address at the driver through the thick plastic partition. Brice took a quick peek at the photo and Russian name on the guy's license, which might as well have stated "Former KGB agent currently hiding out behind enemy lines". The guy seemed to understand the instructions well enough and with a strong "Da!!", he put the pedal to the metal.

As the cab sped off, a warm breeze flowed through the open back windows. All the smells of the city – savory hot dog stands, diesel exhaust, and the like all rushed in at once. Anna grabbed Brice's hand and leaned her head against his shoulder. Brice looked down and breathed her in, closing his eyes in near-ecstasy. They held hands for the entire drive.

The cab rolled to a stop at the curb outside Anna's townhouse. Brice slapped a ten into in the driver's hand and told him to keep the change. Anna jumped out with house keys and bouquet in hand and opened the front door. Brice stood on the sidewalk and admired the rustic stones and wrought iron embellishments on the four-story walk-up. He'd passed it a million times over the years but never really appreciated its beauty.

Anna paused on the threshold, giggling. "Are you just gonna stand there all day or would you actually like to come in?"

Grinning, Brice followed her into the foyer and dropped his bag as Anna headed towards the kitchen. Brice stared in wonder.

The lavishly decorated home, replete with polished

checkerboard marble floors, sparkled from top to bottom. He'd made video deliveries to some pretty swanky places over the years, but this one out did them all. Fred Astaire and Ginger Rogers could've jumped out at any moment draped in a tux and gown and would have fit right in.

Brice's feet drew him toward the kitchen, where he took in all the artwork on the walls. There were black and white sketches depicting scenes from *Bombshells over Broadway* everywhere he looked – 100% one of a kind Hirschfelds, with the name of the artists' daughter "NINA" hidden cleverly in each one.

He'd busied himself deciphering an original handwritten lyric sheet in glass frame when Anna called out to him from the kitchen. "Can I get you something to drink?"

"Sure!" he called back over his shoulder. "Whattya got?" He heard the fridge door open as he walked into the kitchen to meet Anna, who pulled out a frozen bottle of Stoli vodka that looked like it had been waiting patiently under the Siberian permafrost for an eon. Top quality stuff. "That'll work!"

Anna grinned and started whipping up two screwdrivers.

"This is a really beautiful place," Brice said as she poured out the spirits and orange juice into two cocktail glasses.

"Thanks. My dad bought it for my mom when *Bombshells* became a big hit. He told her it was a giant belated birthday present for all the ones he missed when they weren't together."

"That's a clever way to put it," Brice said, and Anna smirked.

"He was a clever chap; no doubt about it." She handed Brice his drink and clinked her glass against his. Brice took a sip and found it the smoothest vodka he'd ever tasted. He and the boys usually had to settle for the rot gut swill they sold over at the corner deli by Max's place. Brice looked back into the living room and asked, "Are those your dad's original lyric sheets hanging up over there?"

"He had some handwriting, huh?" Anna tossed her hair over her shoulder and braced an elbow against the gleaming granite countertop. "My mother used to have to decode it and type all that stuff out for the producers. She used to joke that she could've brought them over to the pharmacy and walked out with prescriptions for penicillin and suppositories!"

Brice laughed and took another sip of his cocktail. A heavy buzz had started to build in the base of his skull already.

Anna put her glass down and said, "Why don't we head downstairs and get you situated?"

Brice tilted his head. "Downstairs?" The image of some sort of strange pleasure dungeon came to mind. This was too good to be true.

Anna took his hand in her own and led him away from the counter. God, her hands were so soft..."We converted the basement into a huge studio apartment," she said as Brice kept trying to keep his eyes off her shapely hips and failing. "That's where me and the gang live."

Brice cocked his head in confusion once again. "The 'gang'?" Now he really had his doubts about where this was heading.

Anna laughed at his expression. "C'mon; you'll see."

As they reached the bottom floor, she whirled on him with a wild gleam in her green eyes. "Are you ready?"

Brice literally had no idea what to expect.

When Anna opened a very tall door and flipped the light switch on the wall, his jaw dropped once again. The neon lights flickered to life with the overhead recessed light, bringing the entire room into clear view. It was akin to a video arcade for adults without the arcade games.

"Holy cow. This is some set up!" Before he could really take it all in, a pride of seven or so cats of all multiple breeds seemed to magically appear from every nook and cranny as if summoned by T. S. Eliot himself. "Those guys must be the gang," he said, laughing at the realization. Anna joined him, kneeling briefly to scratch the lone black cat under the chin. "Yes, this is my gang." Straightening, she pointed to each one in turn and said, "That's Slick, Rose, Murray, Quinn, Fancy, Lovecraft and my oldest, Agnes. Agnes just turned eighteen. She's like the den mother."

Brice looked down as three of the felines rubbed up against his leg in greeting and started to purr. Not the gang he'd expected – not at all – but Brice couldn't make himself feel bad about it. "I'll try and stay on everybody's good side" he said with a wink at the kitties.

Anna checked the glowing clock and gasped. "Oh! I'm gonna be late. Okay," she said, turning Brice toward her by the shoulders "just make yourself at home. There's some wine coolers over in the little fridge. I've got tons of movies, albums, CDs. We've got cable, too, so hopefully you won't get bored." Anna grabbed Brice by the hand and leaned in to give him another kiss.

Brice didn't want to let her go. "Where exactly do you have to go again?"

"Ugh, it's this stupid writer's guild thingy. My mother sits on the board because of my dad, so I have to be there with her to represent the family. It's over at around ten so I'll just jump in a cab when it lets out and be back by 10:30 at the latest."

Brice smiled and said "Okay," and made himself release her hand.

Anna rushed to the bathroom to get ready as Brice sat on the couch. He started flipping through a magazine with Prince on the cover clad in a purple overcoat and matching g-string. Two of Anna's cats jumped into his lap and made themselves at home. "What's going on dudes? Nice place you got here," he said. The orange one yawned and curled up under Brice's arm.

With Anna now out for the evening, Brice found he couldn't keep still. He lit another cigarette and looked for something to watch on cable. There were so many channels, he flipped through them for twenty minutes straight and still hadn't settled on anything.

He sighed loudly enough to make a few of the cats still milling about raise their heads. This had seemed cool in theory, but now, sitting alone in some chick's multi-million-dollar townhouse had started to freak him out a little. Brice picked up the phone on the end table and dialed a familiar number.

Lindsey picked up on the second ring. "Hey, you," Brice said, already relaxing. "What's going on?"

"Oh, Brice? You know the drill, buddy; I'm getting all dolled up to hit LeRoxx."

He figured. "Take a guess where I am."

A smile broke out when Brice heard Lindsey gasp. "Get out! Is she there with you?"

Brice laughed and said, "If you can believe it, I'm here all alone. She had this function she had to go to, so it's gonna be a few hours before she's back."

"Wow, that's friggin' insane. Are you guys vibing or what?"

Brice's heart fluttered at the memory of the last kiss Anna laid on him before she left. "Oh, I'm definitely feeling it."

The spritzing sound Brice heard on the line let him know Lindsey was in the process of dowsing herself in Luv's Baby Soft perfume before she said, "Sweet. Well, sit tight and good luck. I'm sure she's gonna maul you when she gets back."

They both laughed at that and wished each other great night.

Almost an hour passed before Brice let his nagging curiosity get the better of him. It would be at least another hour until Anna would return. With the stealth of a cat burglar, he ventured up the winding staircase to take another look at all that cool memorabilia. In addition to being a literary and musical genius, Garland Miller was also a skilled sketch artist, with caricatures and comic strips lining the walls throughout the house. The sheer elegance of it all blew him away. He ventured up one more flight to find an even bigger eyeful of opulence; rich parquet floors, an antique Steinway piano, and low hanging crystal chandeliers all adorning what could only be described as the grand ballroom.

Brice gave a low, appreciative whistle. They must have thrown some epic parties. He strode over to windows that stretched from the floor to the extremely high ceilings to admire the view when a sudden noise shattered the silence.

Shit, Anna must have arrived home early...he bolted downstairs three steps at a time. This would be way too embarrassing to have to explain. As he rounded the bend, he discovered that Lovecraft was to blame for the heart-stopping crash. He sat atop the bureau licking his paws as the brass pencil holder lay on the floor inches away.

Brice narrowed his eyes at the cat. "You did that on purpose, didn't you? You little bastard...you keep this up and you're gonna need more than nine lives."

CHAPTER 11

Brice was sitting on the floor reading album liner notes when Anna appeared at the foot of the basement stairs and two of her cats sprang up the stairs after one another.

Startled, Brice looked up and said, "Hey! I hope you don't mind. I love reading album credits and you've got quite an insane collection here. Half of these are imports that are out of print. You must have an inside connection."

Anna grinned and continued down the stairs to meet him. "Don't be silly. I just know where to look. Though it is nice to know there are other vinyl geeks like me in the world." She removed her fuzzy pink sweater and plopped down on the floor next to Brice, then leaned over and gave him a kiss on the cheek.

A chill ran down Brice's spine. With a playful smile, she grabbed his wine cooler and took a gulp before speaking. "Sorry it took so darn long. I got outta there as soon as I could. All my mom's showbiz friends always feel obligated to talk my ear off about how brilliant my dad was and how I look so much like him and blah, blah, blah, blah, blah."

"Ah, c'mon. That must be nice, though. I know whenever anybody talks about my dad, I'm all ears. I guess it's because I don't have any memories of him." Brice averted his eyes, glad when one of the cats conveniently walked over to snuggle. The heavy nostalgia came out of nowhere. "Wait – I take that back. I might have one. I just don't know if it's real or if I imagined it or what."

"Is it a good memory or a bad one?" Anna put a hand on his knee. Brice looked up and said, "I guess it's a good one. It takes place in my mom's kitchen in Brooklyn. There's nothing specific about it other than I'm there and he's there. I mean, if it is real, I was only like a year and a half old, so it wasn't like we'd be having a real conversation or anything." Brice paused before adding, "Yeah, one memory and a closet full of his army stuff. "Not a whole hell of a lot.

Anna grabbed his hand. "Well, I guess it's nice for me in a way, but I always feel a little overshadowed by his memory. He left such an impression. There's no possible way for me to ever come close to anything he achieved."

Brice's voice softened with empathy. He sought her gaze with his own. "Listen, you can't go through life comparing your achievements to his. You're gonna find your own niche eventually and that'll be your thing. And whatever it is, I'm sure you'll be great at it."

Reaching up, Anna caressed his face, running a thumb over his bottom lip and leaving it tingling. "You're such a sweetheart," she said. "I got nervous when you didn't call me right away. I thought you had chickened out."

Man, he'd really come close to blowing the whole thing, hadn't he? Frighteningly close.

At least he could laugh about it now. "Yeah, I'm really sorry about that. I guess there's this stupid rule that says you shouldn't call a girl too soon if she gives you her number. You might come off looking like you're desperate."

"Interesting." Anna took another sip from his bottle. Brice didn't miss the bedroom eyes she aimed his way. "I know that, but I thought I may have come on a little too strong asking you out instead of the other way around."

He'd have been lying if he said he wasn't intimidated at the time. "Well, I'll be honest with you...that's the first time anything like that's ever happened to me at the store. You caught me completely off guard."

Anna's eyebrows shot up. "What? I don't believe that for a second. A hottie like you?"

Brice laughed uproariously at that. He didn't consider himself to be a bad looking guy, but he wasn't delusional. He swiveled to face Anna more directly. "You know how people that live in this zip code are. There are very clear social lines and most people don't cross them. To them, I'm strictly bridge and tunnel. I know it and they know it. I couldn't hide this Brooklyn accent if I tried."

Anna shook her head in obvious disagreement hard enough to make her dangling gold earrings audibly tinkle. "Well, I don't see things that way."

Had she scooted closer without him realizing? Brice looked deep into her eyes. "I guess that's why I'm here, huh?"

Biting her lip, Anna gently pulled Brice's face closer with her soft, soft hands and said, "You are here, aren't you?"

"Yes, I am." Brice sensed the deeper meaning behind her question. "And are you sure that's okay?"

Anna's sexy smirk was all Brice could see. "That's very okay."

The two spent a long time drinking, laughing and telling stories about their respective childhoods. Brice was particularly amused upon hearing Anna tell about her escapades with the child movie stars she'd counted as friends. Things they found normal sounded like movies in and of themselves to Brice.

Brice's stories of pre and post pubescent mischief were nowhere near as interesting, but Anna stared at him with wide eyes while he talked like she was fascinated by his boyhood musings nevertheless.

Anna cracked opened her fortune cookie from their takeout and read it aloud: "'Every new beginning comes from some other beginning's end'. She smiled beatifically, folded it in a little square and slid it into what looked like a leather-bound journal she'd taken out of the nearby ottoman.

Whatever question Brice had been ready to ask vanished when Anna eased herself from the floor and walked to the other end of the room. With a wave of her hand, she turned off the room's fluorescent track lighting, leaving just the soft neon lighting under the cabinets in pastel reds and purples. Moving with the grace of a ballet dancer in the dark, Anna glided over to the stereo. She removed an album from its sleeve and carefully placed it on to the soft black felt of the turntable. The crackles and pops of the needle traveling through record's newly minted grooves were crisp and pronounced; the glow of the lava lamp gracing the top of the bookcase gave the room a warm scarlet aura, like an old school bordello.

Brice couldn't stay away if he wanted to. He hadn't realized he was on his feet until he stood before Anna at the stereo, where she held out her arms to him. The guitar harmonics mixing with opening bass and snare drum hits of U2's "With or Without You" filled the room as the two embraced.

Brice already felt way out of his league because of their obvious socioeconomic differences. He knew their age discrepancy could be a dealbreaker at this juncture if he slipped up and accidentally disclosed the truth somehow.

But as the mood intensified, he pushed every negative thought out of his head in favor of surrendering to the moment.

With a gentle finger beneath her chin, Brice raised Anna's head and kissed her with everything he felt in his heart and soul and body. She put on a spunky front, but he could feel the weight of her emotional scars that lay just underneath the surface as they kissed and kissed. That Jamie prick really did a number on her.

Anna needed time to heal. At this moment, Brice knew in his heart of hearts that though he was still in high school and way out of his depth, he was up for the task.

91

Anna brushed aside her silky mane, her eyes and lips fully illuminated as she looked up at Brice and said, "Is this the part of the movie where the 'star-crossed lovers' begin their romantic journey together?"

Brice flushed, caught a little off guard by her wit when most of his reasoning power had headed south, knew he had only a split second to make an equally clever comeback.

He grinned. "I haven't read the script yet, but if I had to guess, I would definitely have to say yes." Stallone would've been proud!

One kiss led to another, then another, then even more. Soon after, the two of them folded themselves around each other, consummating their new bond as Bono and his Celtic brethren wove a befitting musical tapestry for such an auspicious occasion. Warm waves of pleasure the likes of which he'd never experienced before washed over Brice, and he surrendered to the riptide pulling him way past the point of no return.

An hour later, they both lay still, bare legs entwined and basking in the afterglow. Brice took a long drag from a hand rolled clove cigarette and giggled under his breath at the curious stares from her fancy felines.

His life in Brooklyn felt a million and a half miles away. He was well aware that the stress of senior year and the family and neighborhood drama would all wait patiently for him across the river. For now, he gave himself permission to revel in the warmth of this beautiful creature that somehow had mistakenly wandered into his life.

CHAPTER 12

At the behest of his unwavering internal clock, Brice carefully slid out of bed as soon as the sun rose and crept to the bathroom to get ready.

To say that he wasn't looking forward to work was the understatement of the century. The day was sure to creep by at a painfully slow pace given the magnitude of the prior evening's events. As the frosted overhead light went on, he was taken aback by the sheer elegance of the bathroom. With its intricate Romanesque tile patterns, the posh powder room looked like something straight out of a 1940s movie about Manhattan socialites. He'd never seen a bidet in real life before. This one was regal enough to clean the most noble of bottoms.

The clock was ticking. Brice pulled open the heavy glass door of the shower and put the four separate overhead and side spouts on full blast. The lackluster loos back in blue collarville had nothing on this marvel of modern plumbing.

As he washed the last of the peach scented body wash from his face, two toned, slender arms slid across Brice's soapy midsection. The warmth of Anna's small body pressed against his made the eyes roll back in his head as she playfully nipped at his shoulder blade. As he turned around to gaze upon Anna's glistening naked body, his initial urge to plunder such an opulent treasure gave way to his resolute Protestant work ethic which mandated he be dressed and out the door in ten minutes.

With an apologetic and heartfelt goodbye kiss, he scrambled out of the room. He was dried and dressed and out the door in five minutes flat. As he walked down the street towards the shop, he still had a hard time believing he'd actually spent the night in such lavish digs.

As Brice walked into the shop and said good morning to Ted and Rex, he was surprised to see a new face. Ted informed him that Suzette, a pretty blonde from Quebec was between hairstyling gigs and, with her being Ted's new love interest, would now be working part time. Brice certainly didn't have a problem with it. Some new blood would be great. Plus, someone with her thick French accent would be a welcome addition in the foreign film department.

Everything chugged along nicely all morning when Ted pulled Brice aside around noon and said he "needed his help with something down in the building's storage unit". Brice smiled and welcomed the chance to get out of the store for a few and shoot the breeze.

Brice and Ted had always had a great relationship. Ted happened to be a math and statistics whiz and loved bouncing store-related ideas off Brice, who had a more down to earth sensibility. Besides, Rex, Daisy and Suzette seemed to have everything under control.

Ted and Brice exited Video Star and navigated their way towards the Second Avenue storage entrance. The Upper East bustled with activity as the neighborhood heiresses in their pricey haute couture and fashion-conscious pooches meandered down the busy thoroughfare, window shopping and causing every male to pay close attention.

Ted turned to Brice and said, "So, Anna Miller, huh?"

Brice shook his head and let out a hearty belly laugh. "Je-sus! Are you kidding me? It's hard to keep a secret in that little shoe box of a store!"

Ted laughed in kind and said, "What? She's a sweet girl. You guys'll make a nice couple."

Brice had high hopes, but... "Well, that remains to be seen. We're going on our first official date tonight. I'm just gonna take it one step at a time and see what happens."

Ted nodded. "She's a little bit older than you, no?"

"She is. See, that's the thing. I told her I was 21 and now I kind of feel like a heel for lying."

Ted chuckled and slapped his back. "Listen, all's fair in love and war, right? So what's a couple of years? As long as you guys get along, who cares?"

Brice grinned at the sensible advice. Exactly – who would care? Brice changed the subject to his boss' earlier request. "So, what exactly did you need me to help you with? The storage entrance is in that direction."

Ted grinned mischievously and said, "Ah nothing, really...I just really hate eating at the diner alone."

Brice tipped his head back and laughed once more. "Now, that's my kinda help!" Brice and Ted walked into the diner and jumped into an empty booth.

Ted looked at Brice over the top of his menu. "Other than this blossoming new romance, what else is new?"

Brice let out a sigh he hadn't realized he'd been holding in and ran his fingers through his hair. "I gotta be honest, I've had a rough go of it lately."

Ted had the decency to look surprised, though Brice knew he was already aware just like the older man knew everything else. "Really? What's up?"

He didn't know why, but Brice felt the urge to unburden himself. "I just feel lost. Getting kicked out of my Catholic high school for my senior year is still kinda fresh in my mind. My living situation's a mess and I just don't feel like I have a handle on where my life's heading." Brice clasped his hands together on the table. "I mean, look at you. You graduated high school when you were, what? Fifteen? Then you zipped through college in under three years. And to boot, you go on to be the youngest actuary in the history of the state of Connecticut. You must have really had your shit together!"

"Whoa, stop right there!" Ted said laughing, hands up in surrender.

"Yes, academics always came easy to me. I guess it's a family trait. Who knows? And all that other stuff is true. But the fact of the matter is that my teen years, other than the grades, were a complete disaster. Severe acne, shitty low paying jobs, a crummy home life. Trust me, being one of six kids in a strict New England household was no picnic." He took a bite of his breadstick and continued, still chewing. "And look, I wasted all that time and energy to become an actuary and then did a complete 180 and wound up opening a business. Listen, the point is that life's a constant series of twists and turns. There's no way to know what's coming next. It's how you deal with it and adapt to it. That's what determines the outcome." He leaned forward to look Brice in the eye. "You're a tough, smart kid, Brice, and very likeable. I see the way you handle yourself in the store. You treat millionaires with the same ease as you do doormen. That's not something you can teach someone. You either have it or you don't. Just trust your gut. You're gonna be fine. Okay?"

"Wow. Thanks, Ted." Brice, now feeling much better after such an unexpected onslaught of kind words from someone he truly admired, grinned and went back to reading the menu. "You know, you're absolutely right. And there's really no point in arguing with someone who's about to treat you to lunch!"

Ted let out a belly laugh. "Who said I was treating?"

"Oh, my mistake!" Brice said, eyebrows raised. "I guess I'll have to go ahead and tell Mrs. Bandasarian you kinda have a thing for her." Ted recoiled at the prospect and said, "Egads! Order whatever the hell you want!"

Ted and Brice returned to the insanity that was the Saturday afternoon rush. After a full two hours of non-stop action, Brice checked the clock. If Jordan didn't appear in the next fifteen minutes, Brice would be royally screwed.

He was putting tapes away in the back when he recognized the sound of Jordan's unmistakable Brooklyn accent.

He breathed a sigh of relief as he walked behind the counter. Jordan already looked like he'd been sucking on lemons. He pointed a finger at Brice. "You'd better appreciate this. I was kicking ass at Billy's poker game and had to leave!"

Brice looked aghast. "*Poker game*? You told me you gave up gambling for Lent!"

Jordan made a face. "I said I gave up *sports gambling* for Lent. This is poker; it's completely different."

Brice rolled his eyes. Jordan was always splitting hairs. "And you have the balls to stand there in front of Monsignor Sullivan on Sundays and still receive Communion?"

Jordan gave him a playful shove toward the door. "Aren't you late for a date you don't deserve to be on?"

Brice thanked him again and wished everyone else a pleasant evening before he rushed outside to freedom.

Brice bolted towards Anna's house quicker than a newly released parolee. He'd fought the urge to check in with her all day out of fears that he might jinx their plans or even worse, tip his cards. When he caught his reflection in the side window of a parked car, he ran his fingers through his hair like a comb and popped in a fresh piece of mint gum. Then he walked up to Anna's front door, ringing the bell and waited patiently for the woman herself to appear. He readied himself for a giant hello kiss when the door opened.

A statuesque black woman with tiny crow's feet and a flat top haircut like actress Grace Jones answered the door, staring down at Brice from her impressive height with intense blue eyes that didn't look natural.

Had he just entered the Twilight Zone? "Oh, hello," Brice managed to say before his throat completed closed with surprise.

"You must be Brice" she said, her heavy English accent adding to the surreality of the scene. "My name is Isis." She held out her hand.

Shaking himself, Brice shook it ever so demurely. "I'm sorry I look so shocked; I was expecting Anna. Is she home?"

Isis smiled and said, "Yes, love; she's downstairs getting ready. She said for you to come in and make yourself comfortable." She stepped aside, a pleasant little smile still on her face.

Isis accompanied him into the foyer and explained that she occasionally worked for the family on the weekends as a housekeeper and usually kept Anna company when her mother and Mel were in the Hamptons. As Brice headed down the stairs to the basement, Isis grabbed her purse and a shawl from the coat rack and said, "Well, I'm off. Enjoy your weekend and hopefully we can get a little bit better acquainted next time."

"That sounds great." Brice smiled and waved her off.

Anna's lips were pursed in the mirror as she put on her makeup with two purring kitties on her lap when Brice walked in, Prince playing on the record player. He walked over and gave her a big kiss and hug. Brice stood back to admire her cosmetic handiwork. Anna's lips, cheeks and eyes looked striking. She was a dead ringer for a young Greta Garbo.

Brice chuckled and said, "So... Isis seems really nice."

Anna looked at his reflection in her mirror, her eyes all lit up. "Isn't she the best? She's usually around on the weekends when my mom's out of town, but I told her she could have the weekend off. She swung by just to pick something up. Sorry, I should have given you a heads up!"

"No problem. She just caught me a little off guard, is all." At least she didn't seem offended by Brice's surprise at her presence.

Anna got up and slipped her slim legs into the pair of black leather pants hanging over the back of her chair. "When she lived in England, she used to book bands at this really cool club in the east end of London. She used to date Roland Gift from The Fine Young Cannibals before they got all famous."

Brice was thoroughly impressed. "That dude's got quite a falsetto. I always thought it would be funny if he talked in that voice all time. Can you imagine? *'Oh, 'ello!! I'm Roland Gift. Do you know the Queen's English?'"*

Anna snorted a laugh at Brice's terrible accent. "You're too funny. But seriously, Isis is a sweetheart and an amazing cook. Oh, and she bakes the most amazing bread."

"Hey, she had me sold when I heard that cool accent."

All thoughts of Isis fell out of Brice's head once Anna turned around and gave Brice a full view of the finished product. "How do I look?"

Brice couldn't speak. Betsy Johnson and Siouxsie Sioux would be proud. Anna did one final twirl for good measure and asked, "Are we ready for a little *Evil Dead Two*?"

Brice threw his hands up in the air. He was born ready. "Let's hit it!"

CHAPTER 13

Later that evening, Brice and Anna left the movie theater arm in arm with big smiles as a sea of moviegoers poured out into the street.

Anna stopped on the sidewalk to turn and grab Brice's arm, squealing with excitement. "I've never seen that much blood in a movie before!"

Brice laughed. "I liked the part where the hand starts trying to look for its head so he can stick it back on its neck. And then boom! Granny pops up outta nowhere and hacks it to bits with a hatchet! Instant classic!" Brice hadn't expected the movie to be quite so hilarious; it didn't disappoint.

Anna, still doubled over with laughter herself, managed to say, "You'd better make sure I'm the first person you call the minute you guys get a copy in at the store!"

Brice wiped the tears of laughter from his eyes with a thumb before pulling Anna close to his side again. "As long as I get to watch it with you."

"I don't see that being a problem." The smile she offered him practically sparkled as she pulled Brice in for a soft kiss.

As they disengaged, Brice spotted a dirty water hot dog stand on the corner. "Whoa! What do we have here? I wasn't hungry a second ago, but now I'm *starving*! Whaddya say? Are up you for dining 'al fresco', my dear?"

Anna raised an eyebrow at the shabby-looking cart and shrugged. "Well, as long as we don't need to make a reservation, why not? I'm glad I have all my shots!"

Laughing again, Brice directed them toward the cart.

"I was actually gonna suggest Mexican," Anna said with a giggle.

Brice cocked his head. "You know, I've never eaten Mexican food."

"Really? Never even once?" Anna sounded genuinely shocked.

Brice chuckled and said, "Well, I almost did. My aunt and uncle took me and my cousin up to the Catskills one summer for a vacation. My cousin was seriously allergic to parmesan cheese – like it would kill him if he ate anything that had even touched it. Anyway, eating out was a risky endeavor. So we stopped in this place called Chi-Chi's and when they brought the stuff out, I nearly hurled. My cousin gobbled it down, but it looked and smelled like death to me, so needless to say, I've never gone near it since."

Anna just shook her head. "Oh, man – you don't know what you're missing!"

Brice grabbed Anna by the hand and made a beeline to the hot dog stand. Brice perused the steel wagon to make sure there were no health risks and ordered up "two with mustard, onions and sauerkraut". As soon as the complex flavor of the dog courtesy of the heavily spiced "dirty water" exploded across Brice's tongue, he moaned in appreciation. A glance at Anna found her eyes closed in enjoyment, making Brice's chest warm with pride that she responded so well to a little piece of the world he'd grown up in.

It was a perfect night. They walked along the avenue eating their hot dogs and talking.

"So was it really dangerous where you grew up?" Anna looked up at him with huge, curious eyes.

Brice shrugged and tightened his grip on her hand. "You know, for all the bad things you hear about the place, I had an amazing childhood. My neighborhood was pretty safe. There were hundreds of kids everywhere, so you were never bored or lonely. We were free to run wild in the streets as long as we were back in time for dinner. And there were always tons adults around just in case. I mean, you still had to fend for yourself. It wasn't a complete stroll in the park, but you learned all the important life lessons at a really young age."

Beaming, Anna said, "That sounds great. I guess I lead a sheltered existence. My dad and mom were pretty famous, so they had to be a little extra careful. I mean, I'm sure I got to do most of the fun stuff you did, but there was always some level of supervision."

Brice nodded. "Yeah, well...this is New York City. You never know when there's danger lurking around the bend." And almost as if on cue, as the last word rolled off Brice's tongue, a purse snatcher barreled right into them, grabbing Anna's bag and knocking Brice right on his ass.

Anna screamed. Brice was shaken by the sudden event but jumped to his feet quickly. He chucked the remains of his hot dog into the street and charged after the purse snatcher at full speed.

The thief turned the corner off the main avenue and ran down a side street. Brice's adrenal glands opened up like a block party fire hydrant as he tried to keep the culprit in view. Track and field was never his bag. His calves and thighs started to constrict and cramp up with the sudden sprint. The sound of steel trash cans tipping over and hitting the concrete echoed against the brownstone walkups as the pilferer attempted to thwart Brice's momentum every few feet.

Brice was starting to seriously lag behind when he caught sight of an oncoming New York City sanitation truck and its crew. With his last bit of strength he cried out, "Stop that guy! He's got my girl's purse!"

Hearing him, one of the trash crew members picked up a metal lid and smashed it right into the thief's face as he tried to dash by to freedom. Like a scene out of a movie, the evildoer's feet came five feet off the ground before his entire body crashed into the pavement.

As he lay there moaning, the trashman grabbed the purse from his hands and held it up for Brice to see. Brice arrived within seconds, panting like a dog and completely out of breath. He ignored his burning lungs and muscles and looked down at the pathetic wreck on the ground, cracked a wide smile of relief as the good Samaritan placed Anna's bag back into Brice's eager hands.

He was about to convey his thanks for such a heroic gesture and get going when something familiar struck him as they guy climbed back onto his perch on the back of the trash truck. Peering into the man's face and rubbing his chin, Brice said, "Dude, are you from Brooklyn?"

The man wiped his hands on his dark work overalls and nodded. "Absolutely."

Brice's face lit up. "Holy shit! Sal? Jimmy's cousin?"

The guy stepped back and gave him a once over before his face lit up with recognition as well. "*Brice*? Man, it's been a few years, huh? How have you been, bro? I remember buying fireworks for you little bastards up in Bensonhurst. You look great!" Sal jerked a thumb at the would-be thief still moaning in pain on the sidewalk. "What's the deal with this mook?"

"Just some shitball thief with some really bad luck." And no need to involve the cops; the goose egg that guy would have tomorrow would be punishment enough. Brice glanced around for Anna but didn't see her. He must have run further than he'd thought. "Hey man, my girl's probably flipping out right now. I gotta get going."

Sal patted Brice on the back and said, "Yeah man, go do your thing and tell my cuzzo Jimmy he needs to give me a call."

Grinning, Brice reached up to shake his hand. "Sure thing, man.

Thanks again!"

Anna stood a few feet away from an all night newsstand pacing nervously when Brice turned the corner. Both hands flew to her mouth in astonishment as he proudly held up her purse. Like a cheetah in hot pursuit, she ran at top speed and jumped up into his arms. A rapid-fire barrage of hugs and kisses ensued as Brice laughed and tried to keep his balance.

"I cannot believe you got my bag back! But how the heck did you do it?" Brice, was glad she had been too far away to see what actually went down. Not wanting to go into any details that could diminish his thunder, he said, "Let's just say that guy's gonna need a little physical therapy before he gets back into the petty larceny business."

Anna swooned like a distressed damsel freshly rescued from the railroad tracks, grabbing his head with both hands and leaving a lipstick smear across his mouth that would've made the Joker proud.

After a half hour walk home, Brice stumbled through the Miller residence front door with Anna on his back. A good old fashion piggyback ride seemed like a good idea and was par for the course after such a dizzying event.

As Anna dismounted in the foyer, Brice rubbed the back of his neck and said, "I still can't believe that just happened! I thought purse snatching went out of style in the seventies!"

Anna chuckled and kicked off her heels. "Apparently, it's making a big comeback. Who knew?"

Impressed that she could laugh about it, Brice grabbed her by the waist and spun her around once. "What's next? Mood rings? Bell bottoms?"

Anna let her head fall back, revealing her slender neck. "I still have my mood ring *and* my bellbottoms."

"Really? That's so old school." Brice, shook his head. What a night. "A horror flick, a dirty water hot dog and a purse snatching! Talk about a textbook New York City first date, huh?"

Her bare feet soundless on the immaculate marble floor, Anna sauntered over and draped her arms around Brice's neck. "Well, you could say that...but there is just one more thing that would make it complete." She grabbed him by the hand and led the way back downstairs.

Later, as they both lay there in the darkness, Anna's breathy voice broke the comfortable silence. "So...would you actually like to see *Bombshells over Broadway*?"

Brice sat up and happily accepted the offer. Anna got up to find the tape after pulling on a silk robe she had lying around. She popped it in the VCR and hit play. For the next hour and twenty minutes, Brice sat transfixed and saw for himself why the kaleidoscopic masterpiece had instantly became part of the American canon. Every line, every song and every note was perfect. He'd always wondered what the big deal was about it and why every drama department in every high school district in the country put on their own production year after year. Now he had his answer.

Brice was taking his last sip of the wine cooler he'd opened earlier when Anna took out a prescription bottle from the nightstand drawer and dumped a few small blue pills into her hand.

His eyebrows raised. "What are those?"

"Valium. You want some?"

He didn't, Brice picked one up from her offered palm to examine it. Pharmaceutical drugs weren't really his thing. "Nah, I'll take a rain check. You go ahead. With my luck, I'd probably never wake up again."

Anna gulped down a few pills with the rest of her wine cooler before giving him a kiss good night. As they drifted off into slumber, Brice could feel a few of her cats start to burrow in between them for warmth. He chuckled to himself and fell right asleep.

Morning arrived and Brice felt the achy aftereffects of the prior evening's purse snatcher sprint deep in his shins and lower back.

Several of Anna's cats had really dug in deep during the night and had no intentions of moving. The heat from Anna's side of the bed radiated against his back as she remained wrapped in her electric blanket. Brice blinked a few times and squinted, trying to make out the time on the alarm clock display on the nightstand. 7:30 on the nose. Plenty of time for a little more shuteye.

As Brice closed his eyes and drifted back towards REM sleep, he could have sworn he heard a high, lilting voice coming from upstairs.

He must already be dreaming.

As he flipped his pillow over to the cool side, he heard it again. This time it was much closer and clearer. "Anna," the voice called out again.

Brice rolled over and gently shook the shoulder of his slumbering beauty. She cracked open one eye and yawned.

"Sorry to wake you," he said in a whisper, "but someone keeps calling out to you from upstairs."

Anna's gaze went distant as she listened intently, the voice tinged with a southern accident echoing throughout the room yet again.

She closed her eyes. "Oh, that's my mom. I wonder why they're back so early."

Brice pushed himself up against the headboard, suddenly feeling like an intruder. "Is it cool that I'm here?"

"Of course. She knows you're staying with me for the weekend," Anna said on a wide yawn. Movement in Brice's peripheral made him turn him head to see a sleight shadowy figure appeared at the top of the stairs.

Brice's body flooded with alarm until Anna smirked and shouted, "Hello, Mother."

"Hi there, Sweetness. Sorry to bother you so early, but Mel had something come up last minute. We had to get back into the city lickety split," her mother said. She didn't come further down the stairs, but just knowing she was in the very large room made Brice pull the silky covers up around his neck.

Anna shouted her response again, making his ears ring a little. "Okay, I'll be up in a minute!"

As soon as the basement door clicked closed, Anna slid out of bed and grabbed her robe before heading up the stairs. Three of her frisky felines, probably sensing it was high time for breakfast, followed on her heels. "Come up stairs whenever you're ready," Anna said over her shoulder before she disappeared upstairs.

Brice immediately jumped up to take a shower, not even letting himself imagine going upstairs to meet the family matriarch while still covered in her daughter's scent. His stomach trembled at the thought of meeting her face to face in a short time. Though he always seemed to easily win the approval of most of his neighborhood girlfriend's mothers, Anna's mother was an "Uptown Girl" in every sense of the word, having been the darling of Broadway in her own right back in
the 1950s. With no experience on how one should behave in situations like this, he'd have to go on instinct and hopefully not make a bad first impression.

Brice could hear Anna and her mother gabbing away at the main dining table as he walked into the kitchen. Anna put down her coffee cup and gave him a big "Good morning" before making formal introductions. "Brice, this is my mother, Raye. Mom, this is Brice." she said. Her bright smile remained relaxed as she looked between them both, waiting.

With a confidence he didn't feel, Brice held out his hand and said, "It's a pleasure to meet you, Mrs. Miller. I've heard a lot of nice things about you."

The older woman gave her daughter a look Brice hoped was one of approval. "Likewise, Brice" she said, shaking his hand, "and please just call me Raye." When he nodded, she continued. "Anna tells me you two had quite an unexpected adventure last night."

That was one way to put it. Rubbing the back of his neck, Brice huffed a laugh. "An adventure, indeed." Raye poured him a cup of steaming coffee and gestured for him to take a seat in the empty chair next to Anna.

"Oh, I'll tell you, this city's going to the dogs and has been for years," she said. "I just don't feel safe here anymore. But I'm glad my daughter has enough good sense to be with someone who has the guts to handle a bad situation. And not like that wormy little shit, Jamie."

Anna choked on her mouthful of coffee. "Mother!"

Raye just giggled, the thick auburn curls framing her face bouncing slightly against her shoulder. "Anna, it's true. He was a bad apple and I'm pleased as punch he is gone for good." As Brice took a sip of his own black coffee and tried to look everywhere but at them, Raye turned her gaze on him. "I'm sorry to bring that up Brice, but it makes my blood boil when I think about it."

Brice found such genuine kindness and concern in her brown eyes, he couldn't feel anything but amused by her passionate outburst. "No worries, Raye. We all have a couple of chapters in the book that didn't go according to plan."

"Ha! Ain't that the truth." She batted her overly long lashed and Brice sensed she had turned on the charm. "You know Brice," Raye said, "we're gonna have a little bite to eat later and I would love it if you'd join us."

How could he say no?

Lunch was served in the living room, overlooking the backyard garden. Huge swaths of yellow and purple flowers and a concrete Buddha fountain the size of a small child made the place look like the Garden of Eden.

Brice bit into his final piece of quiche Lorraine as Raye went back to telling he and Anna the second half of her favorite Garland Miller story.

"So, at this point, Anna's dad had had about enough. Archie Ward was a big star back in the forties, so he was kinda used to people kissing his ass. Garland had other ideas." Raye gesticulated so wildly with her hands she almost knocked over her glass of iced tea twice. Brice did his best to contain his laughter; a glance at Anna's pinched lips and reddened cheeks at his side told him she was doing the same. "When he wrote words down on a page," Raye said as she continued, "I don't care if Jesus Christ was reading for the part, you were gonna say them his way. So after about five or six tries, Archie looked your dad right in the eye and said, 'you know what I think, Garland?' And Garland said, 'no Archie, I don't know what you think. 'All of a sudden, Archie rips the page in two and says, 'I think I'll use this as toilet paper to wipe my ass with!'" She collapsed against the back of her chair like she still couldn't believe it herself. "Well Anna, your father sprung up like a monkey and proceeded to use Archie's head like a punching bag. It took three production assistants to pry your dad off of the old boy. He stormed off, and that's the last time they ever spoke."

That was a far cry from any of the stories Brice had ever heard about the exalted stars of yesteryear. "Wow, it's hard to believe the kind of shenanigans that went on behind the scenes, especially back then. Seemed like such an innocent time compared to now. I guess a lot of things were just for show."

Raye chuckled in agreement as she took a sip of her iced tea, the satin polish of her manicured nails glinting in the sun. "Yes, it certainly was a different time and place. Oh, well. You can't go back, so better to make the best of the here and now, I always say."

Brice totally agreed. Sure, he had problems waiting for him to come home, but they didn't matter right now.

Right?

"And speaking of the 'here and now'," Brice said, pushing himself from his seat, "it truly has been a pleasure being *here*, but *now* I really have to get going."

Brice went out of his way to thank Raye for all of her hospitality – honestly, he already adored her nearly as much as he did her daughter – as Anna gathered his things and walked him to the front door of her place. She gave him a big hug and kiss and whispered in his ear. "I had such an amazing weekend. I hope you did, too."

He barely had words for how amazing he felt. Laughing, Brice squeezed her and picked her up off the floor, making her squeal in delight. "Are you kidding? Best weekend of my life."

They embraced one more time as Brice walked out into the street, the weather warm and neighborhood quiet as he walked past Hunter College to catch the train back to Brooklyn.

CHAPTER 14

Brice made it to English class just before the second bell, still feeling the sting of having to down plunk 40 bucks of his own money for the graduation cap and gown rental fee. The thought of asking his mother or Aunt Maggie given his educational uncertainty was too much to bear.

Ms. DeLucca, sweaty and wearing a ghastly rayon frock, shuffled around the classroom class handing out last week's quizzes. It wasn't hard for Brice to spot the bright red "F" on the page that cascaded down from her stubby little hands, landing perfectly in the middle of Brice's desk.

He rubbed his temples at the bad news. It did little to alleviate the headache. Oh, God. Brice did have an uncle out in Vegas. Maybe he could find him job in a casino if Brice begged hard enough. Crazy and borderline pathetic, sure, but anything would be better than the daily torment of this slow, inevitable train wreck.

As class began, Brice did his best to concentrate, but visions of Anna, upcoming shows and his mother's outrage with yet another failing grade flooded his mental landscape. He turned the page in *Hamlet* and the words "Whether 'tis nobler in the mind to suffer the slings and arrows of outrageous fortune, or to take arms against a sea of troubles" appeared on the page before Brice's eyes.

That truly was the question, wasn't it? Unfortunately, it was just one in a series of many he still did not have the answer to.

****

Anna insisted on planning their second date after such an eventful first one. Relieved, Brice happily acquiesced to her wishes. It would feel good to leave his brain on a shelf for another evening of bliss with his lady.

She insisted on the evening being a complete surprise. They jumped into a cab and sped across town. As the cab pulled up to the corner of West 45th and Broadway, Brice craned his neck to see the Plymouth Theatre's marquee, which read "Burn This". Supposedly, some actor named John Malkovich was starring, but Brice didn't recognize the name. He helped Anna out of the cab – she looked amazing in her new dress and curled hair, as usual – and said, "Wow, I've never seen a real Broadway play before. This should be fun." Anna kissed his cheek and they made for the ticket booth.

They stood in line for a few minutes with their tickets before the ushers opened the doors at showtime. Brice looked around with mild amusement as a sea of quirky-looking theater geeks flooded the auditorium. The plush velvet seats and gilded floors were a far cry from anything he'd seen back in Brooklyn.

The play itself didn't resonate much with Brice. Anna, on the other hand, seemed to hang on every word. After two hours, they were back out on the street, hoofing it on along Broadway.

"Should we grab a cab back to your place?" Arm around Anna's shoulders, Brice gave her a questioning look. He could think of a few things they could get into.

Anna grinned like she knew all of his naughty thoughts, but shook her head. "No, not yet. We have one more place to go. But I need you to close your eyes first."

"Close my eyes?" Brice laughed. "What the heck do you have planned?"

"You'll see. Now close 'em."

Brice did as commanded and Anna took him by the hand. It took a lot of trust to do this on a public street, risking life and limb navigating through passersby. They walked for about a block and a half before stopping. Anna spun him around and said, "Are you ready?"

His stomach did a nervous flip, but Brice gave a nod.

"Okay...open them!"

Brice opened his eyes, flummoxed at the sight of a giant neon sombrero and the sign above it which read "Santa Anna's Mexican Cantina".

"Mexican Food?"

Anna burst out laughing, her hand on his shoulder. "It's time, buddy. Trust me, you're gonna love it!"

They walked inside and the hostess seated them in a booth right next to a wooden statue of Pancho Villa. The place had a lot going for it in terms of atmosphere.

Anna held his hand across the table, barely able to keep still as she asked Brice if he'd ever had a frozen margarita with salt.

He snorted in disbelief. "I don't even know what that is."

The waiter arrived and took their drink order. The entire time, Brice prayed they wouldn't ask him for ID as Anna gave the mustached server very specific instructions on how she wanted their libations served.

Brice let out a deep belly laugh at the sight of the enormous goblets the server plopped down on the table when he returned. Anna was definitely trying to get him drunk. "Jeez Louise, that's a lotta booze," he said.

Anna chuckled and grabbed a glass of the neon green liquid, so large she had to drag it toward her on the table with both hands. "C'mon, let's have a toast," she said as Brice took ahold of the giant crystal chalice himself.

He cleared his throat dramatically, making Anna giggle. "To Anna Banana, for making me 'see the light'" Brice said, referencing the Todd Rundgren song playing in the background over the restaurant's hidden speakers. Anna cooed and blew kisses as they clinked their glasses together.

The potent tequila concoction went to work quickly on Brice. Within five minutes, he felt warm and numb, enjoying his meal of street-style tacos and rice as if he'd been a fan of this type of cuisine all his life.

Anna, with her small frame, was evidently also quick to feel the magic potion's effects. She hadn't started slurring yet but the words were starting to get warbly. She took a big bite of her chimichanga and winked at Brice, the movement of her eye a little too slow for her *not* to be inebriated. "I think someone might be getting lucky tonight!"

Chuckling, Brice reached for her hand. "Lucky? We'll both be lucky to walk out of here on four legs!" The evening was just...sublime.

As they worked through some fantastic *flan* dessert – at this point, Brice could barely remember his own name, let alone what his dessert was called – Anna told him another story about her childhood, something painful and private he could tell it was difficult to talk about.

Brice was all ears until she stopped and said, "See, that's what's so great about you. I can tell you anything and I don't feel like you're judging me. I hope you feel like you can tell me anything."

And just like that, the joy of the evening burned up like morning mist in the sun. Brice immediately felt horrible about keeping his age a secret. He took another sip of his drink for courage. He zeroed in on her glassy gaze and took a deep breath. Maybe they were both drunk enough for him to confess. She'd eventually find it out at some point, anyway.

He cleared his throat and said, "Listen. Don't freak out, but I have to confess something to you. It's been bothering me for a while and I guess I gotta come clean about it."

Anna put her fork down and with a furrowed brow asked "Confess? What are you talking about?"

"No, it's not anything bad," he said in a hurry.

"Well, then what?"

Brice took another quick sip. Now or never. "You said you care for me, right?"

"Yes...very much." She cocked her head and waited for him to continue.

He let that fact give him strength. "Remember at the video store, when you asked me how old I was? Well, I was afraid if I said the wrong thing, you were gonna reconsider."

Anna's beautiful face twisted with confusion as he blurted out the words he'd been avoiding for weeks. "I-I'm not really twenty-one!"

Anna blinked at him. "Well, how old are you...really?"

His moment of silence before he answered felt like it weighed a ton. "I'm only seventeen."

Her long, heavy sigh made Brice's stomach clench and turn, all that delicious food turning to lead inside his body. She closed her eyes for a long time before she opened them. She finished her drink, her tight mouth giving the impression she was going to get up and leave.

Brice sat on the edge of his seat. Things could go either way.

She did get up, only to slide right into Brice's side of the booth, next to him. She tilted her head slightly so she could look deep into Brice's eyes, which had gone round in shock. She put her hand around the back of his neck, pulling him in closely and whispering, "It's too late. Doesn't even matter at this point because I think I'm falling in love with you."

They kissed for a good long moment before Anna pulled away suddenly, making Brice panic all over again.

"What is it?"

"I'm not gonna go to jail or anything am I?" The corner of her mouth quirked up just before she laughed.

Brice joined her laughter and threw himself back into their kiss.

CHAPTER 15

It was pitch black save for the glow of a baseboard night light when Brice made his way downstairs to the basement.

He'd had a miserable day at school and was feeling particularly toxic and edgy. With his guitar and school books in tow, he could see Anna's silhouette curled up in a ball on the couch. That was...weird. Why was she lying there in the dark by herself?

Something was up. He tiptoed across the room, trying not to step on any of her cats.

"Hey," he said softly when he reached her, "what's going on and why are all of the lights out?"

Anna didn't answer, though she could have slept right through his greeting. He couldn't tell in the dark.

Brice reached under the table and clicked on the lava lamp. As the warm crimson light washed over the room, he peered at her face. Her eyes were puffy and the left side of her face was badly swollen.

His heart jerked in chest. He sat down next to her immediately. "What happened? Did you fall?"

Instead of reaching for him the way she always did, Anna turned her face away.

"No," she said, voice muffled by the couch pillows. There was a long pause. "Jamie came by on his way to work to pick up the rest of his stuff."

That was all she said and all she needed to say.

117

Brice was gonna kill that guy.

Already trembling, his fists clenched as he raised his hand to his mouth and bit down on his knuckles.

That finally made Anna sit up. "Please don't do anything!" She grabbed ahold of his shirt, her voice quivered uncontrollably and only added to Brice's rage. "It was my fault," she said, and Brice couldn't believe his ears. "I said some stupid things and he reacted." She collapsed against him in tears and Brice folded her into a firm hug.

"It's okay." Brice murmured to her over and over, petting her hair as she sobbed. "It wasn't your fault." It took all his strength to maintain such a calm, even tone. Flying off the handle wouldn't help. It didn't stop the visions of a blood-soaked gutter with Jamie's lifeless body lying in it from flashing across his mind like a marquee. He recalled the brutal school yard fights he witnessed as a kid, where the crunch and pop of bare knuckles on skin and skull left welts the size of marbles on the loser's head and face. It was only a matter of time before Jamie would be wearing such a befitting crown. Brice would make sure of that.

The tears eventually subsided. Brice wiped the tears from Anna's puffy face with his fingers as gently as he could manage with shaking hands. "Do you need anything for the swelling?"

"No, I took four Xanex already," she said. Her voice sounded shredded, like she'd been screaming at some point. He helped her lay back down on the couch as he silently plotted his revenge, but he sat next to Anna for another hour until she fell asleep again, holding her hand.

Once her breathing had evened out and he was sure she was just about knocked out, Brice stealthily got up from the couch.

"Where are you going?" Anna's small voice reached him when he was halfway to the door, soft and slurred. "Please...don't do anything rash."

"I'm just getting us some food." He hated lying to her so soon after he'd come clean about his age, but it was a necessary evil today.

She didn't respond and he closed the door behind him with a quiet click.

The setting sun cast long shadows over the Upper Eastside as Brice rounded the corner on to First Avenue. He'd spent the entire eight-block walk psyching himself up for the oncoming brawl and was ready for war.

He caught sight of his opponent in his waiter outfit standing outside the restaurant where he worked.

Completely oblivious to melee coming his way, Jamie casually smoked a cigarette by the establishment's side entrance and kidded around with two Mexican dishwashers.

Brice moved into a doorway and waited for the right moment to strike.

The two kitchen helpers went back in the restaurant and Brice jumped out from behind a parked delivery van. Jamie backed up a step and scowled at Brice. He flicked his cigarette at Brice's head. "What do *you* want, you little pimple-faced shit? To tell me how much you like my sloppy seconds?"

It was *on*.

Brice didn't dignify Jamie's crude statement with a worded response. His grin looked feral when he lunged for Jamie's throat and released a barrage of straight jabs that left his opponent's mouth swollen and bleeding in a matter of seconds.

Jamie, though smaller, was surprisingly quick on his feet and caught Brice with a clean upper cut/left hook combination that almost sent him through the restaurant's plate glass window.

Diners chewing mouthfuls of the early bird special looked on in horror as the two fought viciously, knocking over the outdoor tables and chairs and rolling around on the dirty sidewalk.

It felt like it went on for hours. Brice employed every dirty, lowdown street fight trick he'd ever picked up scrapping in Brooklyn and eventually gained the upper hand. He pinned both of Jamie shoulders between his knees on the filthy concrete. Chest heaving wildly, Brice could barely suck in enough breath to utter a word, but grabbed Jamie by his hair and forced himself to whisper.

"If you ever come near her again, I swear on my father's grave, I'm gonna stomp every tooth outta your motherfucking head and drown you in the East River. Understand?"

All out of words this time, Jamie gurgled up blood and a loose tooth as Brice dismounted his battered body and stalked off down the street. As a final act of defiance, Jamie, writhing in pain, shouted from behind him. *"She's a headcase* man. You'll fuckin' see!"

His words dissolved into the dusk as Brice was stepping into a yellow taxi.

When Brice eventually returned to Anna's basement with a bag of takeout under his arm, Anna's mouth dropped at the sight of his tattered shirt and pants – marginally less distracting than the dried up blood on his badly swollen hands.

She didn't say anything, but the gratitude shining in her puffy eyes spoke volumes. Without a word, Brice sat down next to her with as much dignity as he could and began to lay out the cartons of Asian delights on the table.

He turned to her with a greasy egg roll in hand and smiled, dried blood from a cut lip crusted on his mouth. Anna had tears of joy in her eyes as she planted a kiss on his bruised cheek and curled up against his chest. They embraced for a long time, Brice sucking her sweetness deep into his lungs and holding it in like the finest herb before exhaling.

****

The usual crowd hanging out by the gym entrance was waiting for the first bell of the school day to ring when Brice pulled up in a cab. As he limped towards them, he could already hear the usual suspects starting to his break his balls.

Max jumped up from his usual perch and ran to Brice's side. "Well, well... look who made it in all the way in from the city for his daily dose of public education."

Brice held his side with a wince. It hurt too much to laugh. "Aw, Maxie. You know my day just doesn't feel right without you in it."

Max's eyes widened when he took in Brice's facial wounds and busted up hands. "Jesus, what the hell happened to you?" he asked.

"I had to teach some skell that you never raise your hand to a girl."

Evan wandered over and started giving him a more thorough inspection. He gasped. "Dude, look at your knuckles! If you were looking to scrap, you could have stayed right here in the neighborhood, dummy."

Brice held his side again and begged Evan to stop making him laugh. The morning bell rang as the gang of misfits clad in denim and leather begrudgingly dragged themselves to home room.

Later that afternoon, Brice ran into Jordan on the avenue. He shared Max's concern at the sight of his mangled hands. After Brice recounted the events surrounding the fight, he agreed that there was no other choice other than to dole out an ass whipping.

They decided to grab a bite and as they sat chomping away on their slices in the pizzeria, Jordan smirked and said "You don't actually expect me to feel bad for you, do you?"

Brice barely managed to chuckle. "Jordie, a little sympathy would be nice."

Jordan threw his crust down into his paper plate in mock outrage and said, "Dude! You're banging a hot, rich chick with a townhouse in the city and you're gonna complain? Okay, so you had to get knocked around a bit for the privilege. Boohoo. Poor you. I'd give up a fucking pinky toe to be in your situation. So quit your belly achin'."

Unfortunately for Brice, his friend's tirade was enough to finally bust him up and launch him into hysterics.

Jordan, always a bastion of sympathy, just rolled his eyes. "Good. I hope you fucking choke, ya asshole," he said before ordering another slice.

****

The paper-thin stucco walls of their modest Florida track home did little to protect Brice and his family from the ominous sounds of Armageddon waging on the other side. He, along with his wife and kids, hunkered down in the uncomfortable humidity and darkness of the master bedroom's walk-in closet.

Everyone's nerves were raw. Brice and his wife did their best to keep a handle on the situation. The kids were scared, restless and beginning to become unmanageable.

Brice pointed a flashlight at the radio, twisting the dial and trying in vain to get some better reception. The voice eking through the small transistor speaker barely cut through the sizzle of static. He turned up the volume as loud as it would go and held it to his ear. As expected, the news was grim. Hurricane Hilda was one of the strongest on record in over a decade. Within hours it managed to reach Category 3 status with sustained wind speeds of 125 miles an hour. Roof tiles, garbage bins, lawn chairs and anything else that wasn't tied down all had the potential of becoming lethal projectiles. As with all tropical weather systems of this magnitude, the high pressure mix of hot and cold air had a few additional unwanted byproducts. Intermittent tornados now spiraled throughout the state, adding insult to injury to an already beleaguered population.

With the kid's constant complaints of hunger and boredom, the stress level reached a fever pitch. Brice tried his best to keep cool as the ghostly creaking sound of the home's roof being assaulted by the unrelenting gales began to happen with a frightening degree of regularity.

After yet another complaint, Vera, already frazzled to tears, turned to both kids. "Mara, Caleb...listen up, guys. I'm sorry you're hot and bored, but Mommy and Daddy can't do anything about it until the hurricane passes. And even then, we don't how long it'll be until we get the power back on. I need you both to do your best and not let it get to you. Okay?"

The kids both nodded in compliance, making Brice flash a grateful smile at his wife in the partial dark.

A few seconds later, Brice's daughter tapped him on the arm with her little hand and said, "Poor Tabbie must feel miserable with all that wet fur."

Just then Vera jumped up and screamed. "Oh my, God! The cat!"

She turned to Brice, grabbing his sleeve. "Didn't you let her in?"

What? She was asking *him*? Brice was flabbergasted at this point. "You told me *you* were gonna do it!"

Vera rubbed her temples and said, "I got so distracted with everything else, I must have forgotten. The poor thing is probably scared to death."

Brice's daughter immediately started sobbing. "I want my Tabbie back!"

Taking one look at her crumpled face broke Brice's heart in half. Oh, no.

He looked at Vera and shrugged. "I gotta go get her."

"Are you crazy? It's a Category 3 out there, Brice. You'll get killed!"

Back on fire, Brice slowly got to his feet and said, "I'm doing my best here, hon. Unless you have a better idea on how to get the cat back inside, this is our only option."

Vera breathed a deep, helpless sigh. "Promise me you'll be super, super careful. Okay? If it's too dangerous, please just come back inside."

Brice's son and daughter both begged for him to be careful and told him they loved him in the most sincere voices. Lump in his throat, Brice did his best to keep his tone low and measured. "Alright, everybody just calm down. Everything's going to be fine. I'll just grab her and get back inside as soon as possible." Brice hugged and kissed them all before hastily exiting the closet.

The rest of the home was completely blacked out as he made his way past the living room towards the back patio. The unearthly howls of the outside winds echoed through the house. Brice's flip phone had just enough juice left to provide the dull glow needed to help him find the back sliding glass doors.

He was soaked from head to toe in sweat fueled by anxiety and the relentless heat and humidity. Running on pure adrenaline, Brice knew he had ten minutes at best before complete exhaustion would render him useless. He felt the familiar texture of terracotta tiles floor under his shoes as he reached out for the glass slider. The stainless steel handle met his fingers and he flipped open the latch.

With the glass sliders open, Brice painstakingly attempted to undo the safety lock which held the steel hurricane shutters in place. After dropping the flip phone and fumbling helplessly in the dark to retrieve it, he managed to pry the metal doors open just wide enough to make it outside. As he passed through the narrow opening, the jagged edge of a rusty screw managed to slice him right across his rib cage. The pain was sudden and intense, but he had to ignore it for any hope of finding the family feline alive.

As Brice stepped gingerly out into the back yard, he couldn't believe his eyes. He'd seen his share of the hurricane damage on the evening news over the past week but being in the eye of a storm was a completely different experience. The hot, wet winds swirled with the ferocity of a runaway train, intense and relentless. It looked as if Mother Nature had pointed a leaf blower at Brice's humble plot of land and upended his world.

Brice teetered on the edge of vertigo and did his best to focus. He called out to the cat in five second intervals as he checked frantically behind every bush and tree still standing. What was a pristine manicured landscape yesterday could have been an Orson Welles film noir movie set today. Colossal cypress branches whipped around violently as if in the grips of some possessed entity. Brice had no luck finding Tabbie in the back yard but he was past the point of no return and had to keep going.

Brice cautiously made his way along the side of the house. He crept past the air conditioning unit with its fan twirling in vain and on towards the home's front driveway. Across the street, his neighbor's red Smart Car lay on its side like a discarded toy. His own vehicle he'd covered from tip to tail in a heavy canvas tarp and had avoided any major damage.

Brice started calling for the cat again and froze when he heard a faint meow. The moaning winds made it near impossible to hear anything else. He listened more intently as he called out the cat's name again. He walked over to his car and lifted the heavy soaked canvas, grimacing at the pain from his raw gash, now awash in salty perspiration.

He glanced at his phone – the power indicator showed a mere two percent. Brice held the phone under the car's chassis and scanned for any sign of movement. There in the shadows, he finally spotted her. A terrified and drenched Tabbie meowed and tried to burrow into the metal frame of the tire well when the boom of thunder shook the ground.

With what little energy he had left, Brice got down on his hands and knees and crawled under the vehicle. There were barely three inches between him and the catalytic converter as he tried to grab the cat. She was just out of reach. After numerous attempts she reluctantly crept over and he was finally able to pull her to safety.

Before he could relax his tense muscles and fully stand to his feet, the sound of something tearing caught Brice's attention. There was a brief second of silence, then agony flared like an inferno through Brice's body when a large tree branch came crashing down onto his leg.

The pain took his breath away, but fearing he would scare the cat and lose his grip on her if he howled in pain, he gnashed his teeth instead to absorb the torment.

Time was running out as he felt the last vestiges of strength slipping away into the ether. From some deep, long-buried part of him came the sudden urge to simply close his eyes and accept his fate, but Brice came to his senses before the thoughts could take root. His wife and kids were depending on him to save the day.

He rallied whatever will power was left in his aching shell of a body and committed to coming out the victor. Tabbie was in full on survival mode, digging her sharp talons deep into Brice's flesh. Undeterred, he focused his attention on the parts of his body still functioning. Brice bent his knee and leveraged his other leg to push himself free of the branch. It had to be over fifty pounds. After a solid two minutes of struggling, Brice dragged himself away from the tangled tree limb. He felt a warm trickle of blood snake its way down his leg and looked down. The open wound glistened in the darkness.

With the violent winds now at his back, Brice staggered back to the narrow opening between the hurricane shutters and almost collapsed. With his free hand he began banging on the aluminum like a drum. Within minutes, a wide-eyed Vera appeared and helped him back into the house.

As he lay collapsed panting on the tile floor at last, Brice listened to his wife close the shutters and glass doors behind her. Tabbie ran off to the safety of her bed and began grooming herself as if nothing had happened.

CHAPTER 16

The water flowed over Brice's still-bruised body as he took a quick shower over at Anna's place. Not for the first time, he wondered if he'd gotten in a little over his head.

Though the past few weeks had been mostly great, with both of them spending quality time together in between school, his job and her pulling double shifts at the center, Anna's mood swings were starting to become more and more noticeable. Any little thing could set her off into an inconsolable tirade.

It made him feel horrible, but the words Jamie had flung at him after their fight kept rising to the top of Brice's mind like an oil slick on a puddle.

She's a headcase.

Chicks became a little erratic whenever they got their periods – every guy with sense knew that – but this was different. Very different. More intense and much more scary to witness. Brice had no point of reference to figure this one out.

A few minutes later found him looking through the bathroom's medicine cabinet for toothpaste. Instead, what he found was bottle after bottle of prescription drugs. He grabbed the nearest two and held them up to the light to read the labels. Thorazine...and Clozapine. He knew about Thorazine from The Ramones tune "We're a Happy Family" – a highly potent psych drug they gave to people who were seriously schizo.

Did that really describe Anna?

Only one way to find out.

When he heard Anna's footfalls on the stairs when she returned from running errands, he left the bathroom with one of the bottles in hand to confront her. She'd told him about the Valium, but was she hiding the others?

Anna skipped over to give him a kiss and he held them up, stopping her dead. "What's all this for?"

It was like a storm of anger swept in and Anna snatched the bottle from his hand. She gripped it tightly and turned a glare on him he'd never seen before.

"What were you snooping through my medicine cabinet for?"

It's not like he'd gone looking for it...defensive, Brice snapped back at her. "I wasn't snooping. I was looking for toothpaste and noticed all these crazy looking prescriptions. Who's Dr. Fowler?"

Anna sighed hard through her nose. "He's my psychiatrist."

Damn.

Brice raised his chin. "And why do you have a psychiatrist?"

Anna wilted onto the couch, as if all the fight drained out of her petite body at once. She stared at the floor. "Because I have issues I've been dealing with all my life. The medicine keeps me well. It's no different than if I was diabetic or had asthma." Anna started to get choked up.

God, he was an idiot. Anger evaporated, Brice went to her side. "Hey, I'm sorry. I didn't mean to violate your space. It's just when I opened up the cabinet, I couldn't help but notice. Can you forgive me?"

Anna looked up and wiped her eyes. She offered him a watery smile. "Yes, I forgive you."

Brice released the breath he didn't know he'd been holding. He knew how he could make them both feel better, right now. "Can I make it up to you?" He raised his eyebrows suggestively.

Anna giggled and threw her arms around his neck. "Yes."

****

The sun shone bright as Brice's feelings as he and Anna stepped off the train at Stillwell Avenue. It had been years since Brice had been on the Coney Island boardwalk.

The sweet smell of cotton candy and buttered popcorn blew downwind as the sound of distant screams from The Cyclone, Brooklyn's oldest and most famous roller coaster, echoed against the nearby public housing walls. For a mere four dollars, riders were treated to the most hair raising seven-minute ride of their lives.

Best to get this part over with first. Nerves turned Brice's stomach as they approached the ticket counter. He turned to Anna and said, "You have the distinct pleasure of being the only person to see me on that ride since 1976."

Anna's head fell back on a giggle. "Why so long?"

Brice handed the attendant eight bucks in exchange for two tickets. "Don't laugh, but when I was seven, my uncles convinced me it wasn't a scary ride. Bastards! I was so scared I almost bit through my bottom lip. There was blood everywhere. My mother almost had a heart attack when she saw me get off the ride. They were both read the riot act and forbidden from taking me on any more rides. Anyway, I haven't been on a roller coaster since. I figured it was long overdue and this was the perfect opportunity." He hadn't told that story in long time.

Anna gave him a kiss and said, "I'm sorry if I overreacted at the house. I feel awful about it. You still love me?"

More than anything. "Of course," Brice said. She squeezed his hand as they boarded the rickety ancient-looking car of the ride. Brice put on a brave face as the coaster made its initial five-story ascent, the wood clicking and clacking all the way. He could hear every gear churning as they neared the top.

In a flash, they were freefalling at the speed of sound. Anna screamed with pure excitement at the top of her lungs and kept her hands up through the whole ride as Brice secretly recited every prayer he'd ever learned at church, including the Beatitudes.

They hit Nathan's for a hot dog for lunch. Brice took the opportunity to show her the old CYO Summer campgrounds he'd attended as a kid. A shiny new retirement home now stood in its place. More than once, Brice found himself looking around the place in bittersweet wonder. With a newly renovated boardwalk and tons of revitalization money pouring in, Coney Island was a now a far cry from the crime-infested ghetto that inspired the campy gangland classic "The Warriors".

Nothing really stayed the same, did it?

An unexpected sun shower forced Brice and Anna to seek refuge in a doorway while heading back towards the train station. Soaked down to their socks and shivering, they clung to each other for warmth. There in the shadows of a rundown tenement, they professed their undying love for one another as the deluge raged on. They both made promises Brice knew in his heart neither of them could probably ever keep, but he didn't care. It just felt right.

The downpour eventually tapered off into a drizzle. Anna jumped feet first into a puddle, completely resoaking Brice. She scurried away laughing as Brice gave chase. "You little brat!"

Anna just shrieked laughing as they ran around parked cars like a couple of kids in elementary school.

Anna fell asleep nuzzled into Brice's chest, their train barreling along the elevated tracks back towards Manhattan.

All Brice could do was stare at her beauty with his heart in his throat. He had been too judgmental, confronting her with so much heat about something she couldn't help. She did have a point that mental health issues were no different from any other health issues. His thumb stroked her cheekbone and she still didn't wake. Whether he liked it or not, she had her hooks in deep.

Brice dropped Anna off at her house and caught a cab back to Brooklyn. He wasn't in any hurry to deal with reality, so he decided to stop off to see Max at work.

The Record Emporium was the neighborhood's go-to spot for any new album release and concert ticket purchase. According to Max, the owner's family was connected to the Albanian mob and the place was a basically a money laundering operation. Max didn't care too much; it paid him a few bucks and was a great place to hang out and listen to new music.

Brice found Max and Evan loitering about as he walked through the door. "Look who decided to pay a visit to the common folk," Max said with a crooked smile as he shook hands with Brice. He brought them up to speed on the Anna situation and got an earful of local gossip in return as he and Evan helped Max restock the bins.

Lindsey and the girls happened to be walking by after clothes shopping on the avenue and copping a fat bag of weed. They knocked on the window, all smiles, and came inside. Jimmy The Ticket Guy agreed to watch the counter while they all went outside to the back alley to spark up.

Brice had his lighter ready to go as the freshly rolled blunt got ready for takeoff. Lindsey did the honors and took a good long hit before passing it along. Thick smoke rose up through the fire escapes as they all laughed and chatted about nothing. The general consensus was that this particular batch of Mexico's finest was a little more potent than the usual reefer. Everyone's eyes were reduced to small red slits in no time. Evan attributed it to the unusually heavy rains in the Sinaloa Valley which sent Max and Brice into the usual hysterics. "So now you're fucking meteorologist?" Brice cackled as Max gave Evan a few well deserved noogies on the top of his head.

With everyone now good and high, the group stumbled back into the store, one of them handing Jimmy a big fat roach for his trouble. The store was empty as the friends wandered around looking at album covers.

A chill zipped down Brice's spine as he heard the unmistakable guitar and bass intro of T Rex's "Telegram Sam" bumping through the store's bass-heavy sound system. Lindsey and the ladies started off the impromptu dance party and got down to some serious rump shaking. Even Max stepped out from behind the counter and joined in on the fun. Pedestrians walking by and caught off guard by the curious sight ogled as the group tore it up.

Watching them, Brice found it difficult to remember the hard times.

Why couldn't it always be like this?

CHAPTER 17

Brice made a quick detour from his last video delivery the next afternoon to visit Anna at the center. With his trusty duffle bag in hand, he caught a glimpse of her doing some occupational therapy exercises with one of her students. Anna smiled wide as he approached.

Brice's heart broke at the sight of the little girl sitting in a small wheelchair, but he put on a happy face for the sake of Anna and the girl. "Are you having fun with Ms. Anna?"

The child looked up at Brice and clapped, her innocent eyes making him smile for real. Brice couldn't imagine the amount of patience a person would need to do this every day. It had to really be a calling.

Anna wheeled her back to main area and clocked out for a break. After heading toward the center's atrium, they sat together on a bench under a maple tree. Brice smiled and said, "So, this has to be a pretty satisfying way to spend your day."

Anna looked around, taking in the culmination of her hard work in the patients moving around without assistance. "You have no idea. They are so sweet. And when they hug you, it's the most genuine thing you've ever felt. I swear, I've never had such a feeling of accomplishment before. This is what I want to do for the rest of my life."

Brice grabbed her hand and squeezed it. "See, you were all worried about not being able to finding your place in the world. Funny how things have a way of working themselves out, huh?" Brice looked at her watch and reluctantly got to his feet. "Damn, I gotta bail."

****

Finals were only a few weeks away, looming like a date with the executioner. Painful visions of summer school raced through Brice's head. The thought of having to tell his mother and the rest of the family of yet another failure...he thought he'd be sick.

He checked the clock again on the desk in his bedroom and tried to concentrate on the assigned reading.

Of course, the phone rang.

With a frustrated sigh, Brice reached for it and knocked over the lamp in the process. He was definitely not in the mood for chit chat.

"What?"

"Hey, it's me!"

Hearing Anna's sweet voice, Brice's tense neck relaxed. He pushed a stack of textbooks to the other side of the bed so he could stretch out.

She went on without waiting for him to speak. "So, they're going to be honoring *Bombshells* for its 40th year anniversary at this awards event next week. My mom says I have to be there, so I want you to be my date."

Brice rubbed his forehead. A night with a bunch of high-class schmucks didn't sound like a good time. "I don't know, I already feel so super self conscious around your mom and Mel. This is just gonna shine an even bigger spotlight on me. I don't even own a suit!"

The way she paused told Brice Anna had rolled her eyes. "No problem, sweetie; we can get you a suit. Please? I don't want to go without you. C'mon, it'll be so much fun. There's a big dinner afterwards. We can goof on all the theater swells."

That part didn't sound too bad…"But I got these finals. I literally feel like I'm drowning."

"It's just one night. For me? Please?"

She knew what that tone did to him. Brice knew there was no way he could refuse. He agreed and hung up the phone. He placed the lamp back on the night stand and got back to hitting the books.

The birds were chirping in full force under an overcast sky as Brice and Anna strolled hand in hand along Madison Avenue. Chauffeurs waited in their double-parked limousines, reading the sports section of the New York Post as their affluent employers popped in and out of the exclusive specialty shops. Their destination, Edward's Haberdashery, had been advertising a big 30% off sale all week and the prospects of procuring a suit for the gala event seemed promising.

Edward's Haberdashery. Jesus! That name alone was too cringeworthy to even ponder for too long. Evan and Max would literally cast him into exile if they ever knew.

The store had a serious 1940's Bombay motif happening, which gave Brice the feeling he'd just stepped through a time portal. A sales associate in a snappy navy pin striped suit approached them. The sickly sweet smell of his cologne irritated Brice's nostrils as the man spoke with a thick French accent. "How may I be of assistance?"

Brice, transfixed by the salesmen's sapphire cufflinks, was just about to turn the man down when Anna gestured to Brice and said, "Hi. We need to find him a suit."

The salesman winced as his gaze took Brice in from head to toe and found him lacking. "And…for what type of occasion?"

Anna smiled with all her teeth. "It's for an awards event. We need something…snazzy."

The salesman glided his thumb across his finely manicured nails and sniffed with disdain. "Follow me and we'll see what we have."

Anna and the salesman made polite chit chat as he magically produced a tape measure and took Brice's measurements. Brice was glad for it; he certainly didn't feel like talking to the man.

The next half hour was nothing short of torture, seeing Brice try on an endless array of poorly fitting ensembles, each slightly more unflattering than the next. The lighting and mirrors seemed to showcase every imperfection in his appearance.

Brice was beyond ready to throw in the towel when he spied a modest jacket and pants set hanging on the wall behind a fake palm tree, like someone had forgotten all about it.

He perked up. "What about that one over there?"

Serendipity prevailed, as minutes later Brice exited the fitting room and caught a glimpse of his reflection. He looked relatively presentable and could barely believe his eyes. The last time he was draped in a monkey suit like this was when he, Max and Evan were confirmed by Father Kildare, the notorious drunk of Our Lady of Hope back in 1982.

Anna teased him as the register rung up the final figure. The words "that'll be $388" hung in the air like fog as Brice reached into his pocket. Panicked, he asked to hear the figure again. The salesman, clearly at the end of his rope, outright glared at Brice. He grabbed the invoice and held it in front of Brice's face like a bad report card.

Brice turned beet red from head to toe. He turned to Anna and said under his breath, "I don't think I have enough." Without hesitating, Anna pulled out her platinum American Express credit card and handed it to the Frenchman, who refused to make eye contact with Brice for the rest of the transaction.

Brice and Anna left the shop and started walking back to the townhouse. Neither of them spoke until Brice stopped attempted to hand Anna a wad of crumpled up tens and twenties from his pockets. "I'll pay you back for the difference when I can," he said. He could barely look her in the eye.

Anna looked at him like he had two heads. "What the heck are you talking about? It's not a big deal."

Brice lit a cigarette with a shaking hand. He shook his head at the sidewalk. "That was so fucking embarrassing." Even if he somehow got rich someday, he could never show his face in that shop for the rest of his life.

Anna crossed her arms and huffed. "Why? It's only money."

Only money. Brice wanted to pull out his hair. Of course Anna thought that way. She'd never known a day of want in her life.

He took a long drag from his cigarette and tilted his head back to look at the sky. Blowing the smoke out a long stream from his mouth and nose, he glared at Anna. "That's easy for you to say because you have plenty of it. It would take the average Joe in my neighborhood about two months to save enough to pay for that suit. How am I ever gonna keep up? I don't know how to make anywhere near the kind of money you're used to having." Brice's voice trembled as Anna reached for his hand. Brice looked away.

"Look at me" she said. "I don't care about money. I just care about you. You make me happy. Money just complicates things."

Anna stepped back, her eyes going misty. "When I was little, my mom always used to tell me to be careful because when people know that you're rich they'll pretend to be your friend because they really just want something from you. I know she was just trying to protect me, but I was a kid who didn't know any better. It's really fucked with my head and I've had trust issues my whole life." She bit her lip briefly. "Granted, it's turned out to be true a lot of times, but I let so many really great people slip through my hands because of it, too. I love you Brice, and I don't want you to slip through my hands."

Brice dashed away the salty streams of tears running down his cheeks with his palms and smiled. His heart felt three sizes bigger than it had five minutes ago.

Anna jumped into his arms and kissed him on the neck. She looked up and asked "My mom's staying at Mel's tonight. You wanna hang out with me for a little bit before you get back to Brooklyn?"

Where else was he going to go with her looking at him like that?

Brice slung his stupid Edward's Haberdashery shopping bag over his shoulder as the two walked home.

Later, as Brice and Anna lay together upstairs in Raye's king size bed, he couldn't help shake the feelings from their suit-buying fiasco.

Anna was passed out cold, curled up against his side. He had to get back to Brooklyn soon. The anxiety finally made him slip away to use the bathroom down the hall, but on his way back, he passed a room he hadn't noticed before with the door half open.

A light beamed from the inside. He'd always thought it was a closet or something, but he could see now it was too large for that. Brice could hear Anna snoring from the other room as his curiosity got the better of him.

He pushed opened the door to find it was Garland Miller's private study and froze in shock.

The papers and personal effects on his desk looked like they hadn't been touched in years. Eyes wide, Brice walked around the room examining every inch with awe. There was a large portrait of Garland and Raye over the fireplace and a genuine gold-plated Oscar statue sitting on the marble mantle beneath. He had heard those awards were much heavier than they looked. He delicately lifted the shiny relic and quickly realized it was true. It gleamed despite the fine layer of dust. It must have been a dazzling sight to behold under the Academy Award ceremony lights.

A small upright piano had been placed in the corner of the room with an old seashell ashtray on top of it. Brice walked over and sat on the bench. He raised the worn cover with the utmost care. The ivory keys had yellowed with time. It barely sputtered out an audible note as he gently pushed down on middle C. Who knew what timeless masterpieces were created in this room? It truly was like being in time capsule.

After a few unsuccessful attempts to figure out the opening melody line to Miller's mega hit "You Spring Summer on Me", Brice closed the cover, shut the door behind him and walked back down the hall to say goodbye to Anna. He stirred her gently and said, "Hey, I gotta go. I'll call you later. Anna smiled, told him that she loved him and went back to sleep.

Brice left Anna's townhouse and was about to walk towards the subway, when he figured it wouldn't hurt to see if Gil was still at the store. It was just about closing time and the possibility of a ride home was worth a quick pit stop.

As he'd suspected, Brice found Gil wrapping things up for the day when he arrived. Lori Bandasarian gave him an awkward "hello" as she barreled out of the door with bag of tapes in hand. Brice smiled at her then turned it on his boss. "Hey Gil, don't they ever let you leave this place?"

Gil's eyes lit up. "Brice! What are you doing in this neck of the woods on your day off and at this hour?"

Brice walked behind the counter, grabbed a handful of putaways and said, "I was over at Anna's."

"Ah, the fair Ms. Miller. And how are things?" Gil ran the cash register tape while Brice chuckled and told him, "I don't know Gil. It's complicated."

Gil was too involved with checking the numbers to look at Brice, but he said, "Ah, yes – the trials and tribulations of young love."

"Indeed, Gil. Indeed." Brice put the last tape away with a sigh. "I was wondering if you could find it in your heart to give a poor soul a lift back to the neighborhood? I just don't have the stomach for the train tonight."

Whether Gil coughed or laughed, Brice couldn't tell. "As if you even have to ask me."

Within twenty minutes, they were rocketing along the demolition derby that was better known as the FDR Drive. Gil used every expletive in his repertoire at the procession of tailgating taxi drivers trying to get in his lane to cut him off.

Brice grinned at Gil's colorful choice of words said, "And the rest of the world wonders why New Yorkers are wound up so tight. Have 'em put up with this shit for a week and then get back to us!"

Gil agreed.

"So, Gil...what's your secret?" Brice looked over at him as they headed over the Brooklyn Bridge, Gil hunched over the steering wheel in deep concentration.

Gil tossed Brice a curious look. "Secret? Secret to what?"

"Well, you've told me the story about how when you were my age, you were studying to be an engineer, and then your dad got sick so you had to scrap your plans and go into the family business at the dress factory." Brice could almost repeat the story verbatim. "And then later on, when they opened up the markets with Asia, it basically put you guys outta business within a year. And *now*, having to knuckle it out everyday at the store. I mean most guys would have caved in at this point. But you still manage to treat people with

141

respect and always try to do the right thing." Brice swallowed hard at the vulnerability bubbling up in him, far too foreign to be comfortable. "I've gotta say: for me, not having a dad around to set an example for a lot of things, I've always kinda looked to you for direction. So yeah, what's your secret?"

Gil glanced at Brice with a tenderness Brice had never seen. "Brice, I guess what it boils down to is that I know who I am and I love my family. Once those two things are firmly in place, it just makes life a whole lot easier to deal with."

Brice appreciated the answer – short and to the point, much like the man himself. He nodded, taking it in. "Yeah...yeah. I guess it does."

CHAPTER 18

Anna was bouncing off the walls trying to get ready for the big event. Brice's pleas for help with his tie fell on deaf ears as he stood before the mirror in her bathroom in his brand new suit. It had been years since parochial school required him to master the fine art of the half Windsor knot.

Raye called down in sixty second intervals, giving ample warning of the stretch limousine that was on the way. Anna rushed by to get her high heels from the closet and said, "Wowza, you clean up nice."

Brice was on his third attempt at tying his tie when he looked into the mirror and said under his breath, "I can just hear it now...we're going to walk in there and the announcer will say, 'Ladies and gentlemen, please welcome The Miller family...and some teenage idiot who has no business wearing a suit or even being here for that matter!'"

Anna shook her head and had his tie done in twenty seconds, leaving Brice staring at her in awe once she had whirled away again to finish getting ready. "Where the hell did you learn how to do that?"

"By watching my mom and Mel. Too bad you're not wearing cuff links. Those are fun." She winked at him before taking a moment to put the finishing touches on her already perfect face. "How do I look?" she asked as Brice put on his suit jacket. "Like a super model," he said with a grin as they headed upstairs.

Brice cringed at the sight of Anna's newly acquired Rex painting that hung on the wall. He'd held his tongue in the interest of keeping the peace, but made a mental note to read his coworker the riot act for such a sneaky move.

The white stretch limousine was idling outside the house as Anna, Raye, Mel and Brice stepped out in all of their finery. They were off in a flash.

The Lincoln Center was lit up like a Christmas tree for the event. As their vehicle turned off into the arrival area from Columbus Avenue, the butterflies in Brice's stomach started to riot. Reporters and photographers from *Playbill*, *The Times* and *The New Yorker* all waited behind police barriers for Broadway and entertainment royalty to arrive. Raye and company exited their rented pleasure craft and were met by the show's organizers. Cameras flashed as they were led to the main staging area.

Brice turned to Anna and said, "Man, this is really over the top." Nothing could have prepared him for this kind of scene.

Anna laughed. "Just keep smiling. Who knows; you just might get your picture in the morning edition."

They stood in front of the fountains surrounded by a sea of eager onlookers for what seemed like an hour as the press snapped picture after picture. Minutes later they were whisked to their seats.

Brice's throat ached with thirst as he and their group walked into the after party banquet area once the main event had concluded. A jazz quartet played Muzak versions of the great American songbook. An hour and a half of award speeches, heartfelt recollections and a full-on Garland Miller career video retrospective had Brice's head spinning. The schmooze Olympics were about to get under way and he wanted to make sure he was buzzed enough to get through the second leg of the night.

End to end catering stations lined all four walls of the large room and smartly dressed cocktail servers weaved through the crowd with practiced skill. After leaving Brice briefly for some official family photos, Anna broke away from Mel and Raye to return to his side. "Now that wasn't so bad was it?" Her eyes sparked like gems in the low light.

Brice still felt too uptight to admire them for long and loosened his tie. "I think I need a drink; I'll catch up with you in a few."

The bar line was only two people deep. Brice ordered a screwdriver and got down to business. Anna was preoccupied, chatting away and catching up with old acquaintances, so he opted to hang back and blend into the scenery.

One drink turned into two, which turned into five, and before he knew it, Brice was officially drunk off his ass. His last deep plunge into the vodka and orange juice swimming pool was years ago at a party that had left him half conscious and slumped up against an abandoned car in a church parking lot. He needed to hit the brakes on the libations and coast a bit before things got ugly.

Grabbing a couple of hors d'oeuvres off a slow-moving silver platter, he leaned up against a nearby wall for support. Anna waved from across the room to make sure he was okay, just far enough away not to realize how shit faced Brice had already become.

A tall, stately woman wearing a shimmering black evening gown and pearls smiled at Brice with immaculate teeth and asked if he was having fun. Brice just raised his glass and gave her a smile. He didn't trust himself to speak.

Brice could see Anna approaching and decided to meet her halfway. He took a deep breath and tried to keep it together as gravity did its best to knock him down. Anna, with glass of wine in hand, gave him a peck on the cheek. "Uh, take it easy tiger. I don't want you winding up with a lampshade on your head."

Giggling, Brice took a sip from his now lukewarm cocktail and mumbled, "Never you mind, my little social butterfly, I'll be fine."

"Oh, there's someone I want you to meet. An old friend of mine. I think you two would get along great." Brice raised his glass and slurred. "Great, bring him on over."

As he waited for the introduction, an older matron tapped him on the shoulder and asked if he could help her locate her diamond earring that had fallen on the floor. He cautiously stooped over and picked it up. He tried hard not to think about the fact that the huge diamond probably cost more than Uncle Amir's car.

As he handed it to her and she thanked him, he felt another tap from behind. He turned to find Anna and a young, svelte chap in a tuxedo standing arm in arm. Anna looked up at him and said, "Brice, I want you to meet a very dear friend of mine."

Without thinking, Brice held his hand out – then froze when he saw the friend's face.

That "dear friend" was the guy in the pink Lacoste shirt from the video store who had mercilessly belittled Brice, who suddenly couldn't feel his face.

Of course, Anna had no clue about the event and continued on with the formal introduction. "Brice Laine, this is Graham Covington."

Graham, also making the connection, sneered and held out his hand – palm down, like he expected Brice to kiss the ornate gold ring he wore on his middle finger. Probably a family crest, or some shit. He looked Brice in the eye, his mouth curling into a smirk. "It's an absolute pleasure." Graham squeezed Brice's hand tightly, stood back and looked him up and down before saying, "That is really a *nice* suit."

Nothing about his tone made Brice believe a word of the nastiest compliment he'd ever heard. Anna gave Brice a playful smack on the chest. "See, I told you it was nice!" She shook her head at Graham. "He didn't want to believe me."

Lightning could have struck him right at that very moment...Brice was dying inside, but given his inebriated state, he didn't want to ruin the evening by causing a scene.

146

And Anna just wouldn't stop... "Graham and I have been friends forever. We were even high school sweethearts for a little while, but I got sick of the competition!"

Graham chuckled mildly at the comment but continued staring a hole through Brice. Raye called out for Anna to come say hello to a few people. She took a sip of wine and said, "Okay, you two – I'll be back in a minute" before running off once again.

Brice's stomach roiled. He couldn't feel his feet, now. The stupid suit suddenly felt like it had been crafted from steel wool instead of linen.

Pink Shirt was the last person he'd ever expected to see here, but Brice had to admit now that he was also the last person he wanted to see.

He stared at Graham. Graham just cocked his head and stared back, like Brice was an interesting exhibit at a museum.

Fuck this.

Brice turned on his heel to walk away when Graham stepped in front of him and said, "Well, well...it's amazing who they actually let slip into these functions. I guess poor Anna's been reduced to taking in stray video clerks. My God, that *really* is a great suit."

Brice couldn't breathe or speak or blink or think.

Unhurried, Graham took a delicate sip from his champagne glass with slitted eyes before he smiled like Brice imagined a venomous snake would if it had been able. "You want to take a swing at me right now, don't you? I can tell. Yep. You wanna smash my fucking face in. But you won't. Because you see what'll happen is..." he trailed off, making a show of looking around the room. "What will happen is you'll show everyone in here, including Anna, Raye and Mel, that someone like *you* really doesn't belong here." He dared to step closer, so dangerous when Brice was already seeing red. "See, no matter how much you try, you just can't hide what you are. And we both know what *that* is. But hey, who knows? Maybe true love just might conquer all."

Breathe. Brice just needed to breathe and he could get through the rest of this...toxic speech full of upper class bullshit.

"Well, I gotta get back," Graham was saying. "It's been a real pleasure chatting with you, *Brice*. I'm sure we'll see each other again next time I get bored and decide I want to rent a video. You have a great night."

Brice, still overly imbibed, found himself paralyzed as the coldhearted words hit home, triggering every insecurity he'd ever had, but after Graham walked away, he turned to give one last parting shot: "Oh, and by the way – she gives one hell of a blow job."

It felt like a knife twisted in Brice's chest, right in his heart.

Brice had had enough and practically ran for the side doors. He burst out into the main lobby, grinding his teeth holding back hot, prickling tears of shame. Barely able to breathe, he struggled to undo his tie and find an exit sign.

Anna, who must have been on her way back to him when he left, followed behind a moment later, calling his name. "Brice, where the hell are you going?"

In the middle of the lobby, Brice whirled as she approached and screamed the words so forcefully his throat burned: "I'm going *home*!"

Anna ran full speed in heels to catch up with him, grabbing his arm to make him stop and look at her. "What just happened? What's going on?"

He stood there trembling and tried to catch his breath. "I'll tell you what happened. That fucking cocksucker 'dear friend' of yours just gave me some very valuable advice. He said you can't hide what you are, and he's right. I can't. I'm a seventeen-year-old fuck-up from the wrong side of the East River who has no business being at an event like this." He gestured angrily at his suit. "Look at me. I look like a fucking joke and I feel like an even bigger one. Am I really the best you can do?"

Anna's mouth worked like a gasping fish, her eyes shining with unshed tear. "Yeah, well, then I guess we're both fucking jokes. I gotta go."

Brice ran outside to the street before she could stop him again and tried to get his bearings. He still couldn't think straight and his hot skin felt too small for his frame. A bum pushing a grocery cart asked him for some change. Brice handed him a dollar bill and continued towards the Columbus Circle station to catch the train back to Brooklyn.

It was the longest train ride of his life. The majestic downtown skyline sparkled with a million lights as they passed over the bridge. It was cold comfort after an evening of having his soul crushed to pieces.

Aunt Maggie and Uncle Amir were already asleep as Brice crept in through the front door and made his way through the darkness up to his room by memory. He shucked off his suit and kicked the whole thing into a dark corner before crawling into bed.

Were things ever going to get better? As soon as he had the audacity to think they could, life always slapped him back to reality.

He reached over to turn out the light and noticed the blinking red light on his answering machine. His throat closed with emotion as he lowered the volume and pressed play.

It was Anna. Her voice was hoarse as she spoke, like she had been crying. "Hey. It's me. I'm so sorry about tonight. I know you probably hate me, but I had no idea things would turn out that way."

She sighed, long and hard. "Graham, that fucking asshole. I threw a big glass of red wine on him in front of everyone. My mother almost had a heart attack. I gotta work at the center tomorrow, so I'll stop by to see you at the store afterwards. Hopefully we can talk. I love you."

Still feeling like a raw nerve, Brice closed his eyes and waited to drift off to sleep. It took a long time that night.

CHAPTER 19

The following morning, Brice had a throbbing hangover and could barely keep his eyes open in all his classes, but as usual, English was the worst. He'd had about enough of Hamlet and secretly wished Shakespeare had killed him off in the first act.

The bell rang just as they were getting to Ophelia's watery demise. Brice gathered up his books and started walking towards the door. Ms. DeLucca looked up from her desk and said, "Hey Brice, would you stick around for a second? I need to speak with you."

Shit. No way was he going to get good news.

Once everyone had filed out into the hall, Brice approached her desk feeling like he was headed to a firing squad.

"Have a seat." Her chubby hand gestured at the broken desk nearby. Brice slid into the seat and stared at her with wide eyes, waiting for his doom.

"I've got some bad news kiddo. I've given this a lot of thought and you're just not going to make it this go-round. Even if you ace the final, there's no way I can pass you with these grades. I'm really sorry, but it's just not fair to the other students who've put in the work."

One breath in, one breath out. That's all Brice could do. What the hell could he say? Any rebuttals at this point would be an exercise in futility. With a stiff nod, he grabbed his belongings and fled the classroom.

A dull ache coursed through his entire body. He was truly at his breaking point.

Since they usually walked to class together, Max was already waiting for him in the hallway. His buddy took one look at Brice's stricken face and pulled him aside near the lockers.

"What's wrong?"

Brice could barely get the words out. It took him a couple of tries, but he said, "I'm completely screwed; that's what's wrong."

"Whaddya mean? English class?"

Brice nodded and could have sworn he felt a noose around his neck. "She said no matter how well I do on the final, she's still gonna fail me. I managed to scrape by in every other one of my classes. Even math, if you can believe it. Fucking English? You gotta be kidding me!"

Even Max seemed at a loss. He put his hand on Brice's shoulder and said, "I'm sorry, man. Wish I could help."

Brice faked a smile for his friend's benefit. "Thanks man. Sorry to unload all of my shit on you. Let's just get outta here. This place makes me sick."

****

It was getting close to quitting time at the shop and there was still no sign of Anna. It had been one of the worst weeks of Brice's life, so maybe her not coming in was a good thing.

He had almost finished putting away the last bunch of tapes when Isis walked through the door, her forehead creased with a deep frown.

"Hey Isis," he said, walking over. "Where's Anna? She was supposed to stop by."

"Hello, Brice." Brice was struck by how strange her accent sounded in the shop. "Could we...talk outside for a moment?"

"Uh, sure." Brice held the door open for her and lit a cigarette as Isis began speaking. "There was an incident with one of the older kids at the center. Anna got caught in the middle of a fight or something and they put her on temporary suspension. She's devastated."

Brice flicked his unfinished cigarette into the street and rubbed his head in disbelief. Now Anna could lose her job on top of everything else?

"Are you kidding?" Brice threw his hands up. "If I hear any more bad news this week, I'm going to have a nervous breakdown...what actually happened?"

Isis shrugged and said, "They don't know, but they have to do an investigation, and by law she can't interact with any of the kids until it's done." If it were possible, Isis' expression sobered even further. She clutched her hands before her. "Listen, Brice. I love Anna and I would never speak ill of her. But the truth of the matter is that she has some serious emotional and psychological issues she's been dealing with for years. It has absolutely nothing to do with you. The longer you stick around, the harder it's going to be on both of you if the situation starts getting really bad."

She's a headcase...

Brice shook his head to once again dislodge Jamie's parting words and took a deep breath. "Listen Isis, I truly appreciate your concern and I know you're only saying this with the best of intentions. And trust me, I've thought about throwing in the towel and bailing out on her, but...something just won't let me do it."

Isis inclined her head. "Well then, I guess you've got to follow your heart." Her accent really made it sound like they were acting in a poignant movie scene.

"I'm going to stop by after work," Brice said. Anna needed him. He was surprised when he reached out and Isis allowed him to pull her into a hug. She patted his cheek with a fond smile before she went on her way.

Brice stood outside the townhouse a short time later and rang the bell. Raye opened the door without saying a word as he walked in. The tightness around her mouth said it all.

Brice found all the lights dimmed in the basement as he trudged downstairs, Anna lying under a blanket on the couch – her favorite spot. Today, her miniature pride of cats surrounded her as she stared blankly at the TV.

As Brice walked over and gave her a kiss on the forehead, he didn't miss the open bottle of tranquilizers on the table. She'd spent the better part of the day numbing the pain.

Sad eyes looked up at him, their color muted. "How does it feel to date someone who's cursed?"

Brice chuckled sadly. "I was going ask you the exact same question."

She cleared her throat multiple times, as if she hadn't spoken in a long time. "I'm serious. You, my cats and working at the center with the kids are the only things that bring me any joy. And now one of them is gone. Something like that only happens to someone who's cursed."

Brice sat close enough for their legs to touch and gave her a tight hug. "Listen. I'm going be honest: I don't have any words of wisdom that will make you feel any better right now. Just know that I love you and this awful feeling will eventually go away."

Anna sighed and rolled over. She entwined their fingers and sniffled.

"How about this?" Brice leaned closer to get her to look at him. "You're coming out with me and my crazy Brooklyn crew this weekend and I'm not taking 'no' for an answer. My friend's band is playing their first show at LeRoxx. We'll have a blast and we can get our minds off all this awful shit."

Anna was already falling asleep and barely mumbled an audible response. "I don't know. Maybe."

Brice stopped by his grandmother's house to lick his wounds and sleep off the remnants of such a wretched day. He dozed off on the couch as she sat in her recliner happily knitting, once again listening to Eydie Gorme' sing the Spanish songs she grew up on.

Granny's voice was salve for Brice's soul, retelling all the stories she told him as a child: coming to America, struggling to survive on the Lower East Side, and his favorite – the one where his great-grandfather went to war with The Black Hand. That was always a gripping tale. Brice watched her joyfully knitting away and felt a little better before finally succumbing to sleep.

Brice and his mother had been avoiding each other for obvious reasons. The news that he'd failed to make the cut for graduation was like a dagger through her heart. He was surprised when she suggested they both go out to their favorite restaurant for dinner the next day.

Brice had just given the waiter his order when she looked him in the eye, folding her hands atop the table the way she did whenever she needed to say something important.

She tossed her long black hair over her shoulder. "Okay. Before we get into anything, I just want to say I'm willing to admit that I may have been flying off the handle lately, but you have to realize something, Brice. I'm your mother. I can't sit there and not say anything when I see you going down the wrong path."

Brice's arms crossed over his chest and he sat back. Was she trying to make him feel worse?

"It cost a lot of money to send you to a private high school," his mother said, "and to watch you throw it all away and not be able to finish out your senior year there...it broke my heart."

Brice opened his mouth to protest but she raised a hand to stop him.

"Let me finish. It would be one thing if you didn't have the 'ability' to do the work. But that's not the case and you know it." This time, his mother sat back in her chair. "That being said, I went back up there today and talked to your English teacher... again."

Brice's heartbeat skidded to a stop. "You did what?"

"You heard me...and guess what? I got you one..last..chance!"

He had to be dreaming. "You're kidding! But she told me it was over and that it wasn't even worth taking the final."

His mother took a sip of wine, a smug little grin tugging at the corner of her mouth. "Yeah, and that's where it would've stayed had I not gone up there and thrown myself at her mercy. She said, and I quote: 'if he can pass the final, he'll pass the class'. And then you graduate with everyone else."

Having become so used to feeling awful, Brice was flabbergasted. His throat tightened when he watched his mom's eyes soften and she said, "Grandma did the same thing for me at the end of my senior year, so I figured it was my turn to do it for you."

Clearing his throat, Brice gave her an incredulous look. "Get outta here...Grandma did that for you?"

Chuckling, his mom nodded, a bit of mischief sparking behind her eyes. "It's a long story, but yes. She marched into my science teacher's classroom and wouldn't leave until he agreed to let me take the final over and graduate on time.

Brice burst out laughing. "Man, she's a tough little broad."

His mother agreed then said, "That's pretty much it. Don't blow it 'cause there ain't another second chance to be had. Now, give me a hug and a kiss and a great big "thank you" so I can order. I'm starving!"

CHAPTER 20

Anna's case at the center was still under review, leaving her teetering on the edge of a complete breakdown all week. It took a while, but Brice was able to persuade her to accompany him and the gang to finally see a show at LeRoxx.

Anna got all dolled up and really looked the part. Her lipstick and blush perfectly complimented her fishnet stockings and stiletto pumps. After a harrowing sojourn along the Brooklyn Queens Expressway, Brice and Anna jumped out of the cab an hour later under the elevated subway station and walked towards the club.

Brice caught sight of Max, Evan and Lindsey, who waved him over to a choice spot on the line. Brice introduced her to everyone, pride puffing up his chest. Evan, in typical hambone fashion, kissed her hand like she was royalty and did some weird genuflection. Lindsey just gave her a huge hug and immediately said, "Oh my God, I love those earrings!"

Anna blushed and smiled demurely. "Thanks. I bought them at this little place in the village called Quantum. They hand make all their stuff. It's a really cool shop."

Lindsey swatted Brice in the ribs with the back of her hand and said, "Wow, Brice. She's got really great taste...in jewelry!" Brice laughed as the line started moving.

There was barely room to turn around in the crush of human flesh they found inside the building. Brice went to the bar to score some drinks for everyone as Anna chatted up a storm behind him. Bob Rock was holding court with a couple of rocker chicks and gave him a nod. He touched the side of his nose to see if Brice was in need of some speed. Brice laughed to himself and just shook his head.

Grant and Dana came over and introduced themselves to Anna. The energy in the room felt electric. This was Tristan's first gig with his new band and everyone was excited to see him in action.

Brice made it back just as the house lights dimmed. The gravelly voice of the club's DJ, "Mike The Menace", came roaring through the PA system. Screams of anticipation broke out as he spoke: "Happy Friday, all you pretty boys and girls! Welcome to the world-famous LeRoxx night club, representing the toughest of all the five boroughs – Brooklyn!!!"

The crowd really started going wild as he continued. "We've got a jampacked evening of rock and roll for all of you lunatics, and here to kick things off in a decibel range not for the faint of heart. Ladies and gentlemen, let's make some noise for Mother's Destruction!"

Fists went high into the air as Tristan's new band rocked the place for a solid thirty-five minutes. It was a total love fest as Brice and his crew banged their heads to the spectacle. Even Anna seemed thunderstruck by the performance, her eyes wide and mouth open on a continuous scream the entire time. Brice grinned knowing she had put her worries and anxieties into cold storage for the night.

The group spilled out onto the street after the show. In honor of Tristan's stellar debut performance, they all agreed HQ would be the after party spot. As they all walked towards car service, Brice joked around with Lindsey and her crew and noticed Anna acting a little distant, standing off to the side a little apart from the rest.

"Hey," he said, sidling up to her, "is everything cool?"

Anna didn't answer, but she did offer a half smile and took his hand.

HQ was rocking in full effect as the after party got underway. All the usual suspects piled in as the room inched closer to maximum capacity. Pills, booze, smoke and blow all flowed freely.

159

Brice tried to give Anna some breathing room to connect with some of the guests as he did some shmoozing of his own. Max walked over to him and yelled in his ear to be heard above the booming bass. "Thank God my folks love that damn country house. If they knew for a second what goes on when they leave, they'd padlock the place until they got home!"

As Brice threw his head back and laughed, he caught a glimpse of Anna chatting it up with Tristan. She had been pounding drinks nonstop and was starting to get noticeably hammered.

After working his way through the crowd back to her side, Brice pulled her aside and kept his voice as low as he could. "The night's young, you might want to slow it down a little."

He hardly recognized the girl who looked up at him with a snarl. "Who are you? My fucking mother?"

Brice was taken aback by her Jekyll and Hyde transformation. He tried to snatch the cup from her hand but she held on to it. "Hey, I'm serious. Take it down a notch."

Anna yanked her arm away and said, "I'm gonna go talk with Max's brother, if that's okay with you?" With a sneer, she turned away.

Seething, Brice walked over to Evan as she and Grant started talking in the corner behind a bunch of couples grinding to the music.

Twenty minutes later, as Brice left the basement bathroom, Tristan ran up to him and said, "Dude, I think it's time for you to take your friend home. She's completely fucking obliterated and Grant's girlfriend is getting super pissed off."

If it wasn't one thing, it was another. Brice rolled his eyes. "Fuck me..." He ran upstairs, and when he found Anna in the living room, he couldn't believe how drunk she'd allowed herself to become. Her legs could barely hold her upright and Grant was trying to keep her steady without touching her too much. She saw Brice making his way across the room towards her and then did the unthinkable: she grabbed Grant's head with both hands and jammed her tongue into his mouth.

All hell broke loose. Grant's girlfriend, Dana, lunged at Anna screaming "Get your fucking hands off my boyfriend!" Grant was in a complete state of shock and pushed her away as hard as he dared, Anna's lipstick smeared across his mouth.

That was the last straw. He did not invite Anna there with his people and his friends to make a fool out of him. Brice grabbed her by the arm to get her outside.

She broke free and shrieked. "Get your fucking hands off of me!" before letting out a high-pitched, blood curdling scream.

The entire room went silent. Someone even stopped the music.

Anna stood there against the exposed brick wall trembling, her chest heaving. Realizing what had just happened and with everyone staring at her in disbelief and bewilderment, she tucked her clutch purse into her armpit and ran out the door, bolting into the street before she disappeared.

Brice stood there with his mouth agape, staring at the space she'd just vacated. Max and Evan ran over. Brice was dumbfounded. The presence of his friends at his side reanimated Brice enough for him to walk over to Dana, who was beside herself and wiping the lipstick from Grant's mouth. "I am so fucking sorry," he said. "I have no idea why she acted that way."

Grant shrugged. Brice knew it wasn't the first time a drunk chick had thrown herself at him and it wouldn't be the last. "No worries, man, but she's gonna get hit by a car if you don't find her and get her back home."

Mortified and worried, Brice pushed his way through the crowd and bolted from the house to find Anna. He dashed off in blind pursuit, looking everywhere for a clue to where she could have gone.

He turned the corner and saw her stumble onto the main avenue. He sprinted as fast as he could to catch up with her. Anna was stumbling in and out of traffic looking for a cab back to the city as he drew near. The blowout and cool evening air seemed to have sobered her up a bit; she was a little less unsteady on her feet.

"Anna!" He called out to her a few more times, but she didn't respond.

Brice finally caught up to her and said, "Slow down, you're going to get hit by a bus!"

Glaring, she pulled away and said, "Just go away. I want to go home!"

"What the fuck just happened in there?"

She kept walking and yelled back at Brice over her shoulder. "I don't want to talk about it!"

Enough of this.

Brice ran right into her path and stopped her, grabbing her by the shoulders to keep her still, if only for a moment. "Well, if you were trying to hurt me, mission accomplished! What could I have possibly done to make you pull a move like *that*?"

Anna began to tear up, which confused Brice even more. "You completely fucking ignored me all night," she said, voice trembling, "and to make matters worse, I have to stand there and watch you and your little gal pal Lindsey rub it in my face."

Brice was dumfounded. He had done his best to make her feel part of the crew. He must have really fallen short to cause her to act out like that.

162

"Rub it in your face? Lindsey? What the hell are you talking about? There's nothing between us other than a good friendship. And I did my best to include you, but you didn't seem that into it. I'm sorry if I made you feel like an outsider. It wasn't my intention. I wanted to get your mind off the whole center thing you've been dealing with." Brice's arms dropped to his sides in defeat. "Man, I've really had some shit luck lately. I guess this is just a continuation of my losing streak."

Shivering, Anna licked her lips. "I just made a complete idiot out of myself in there and I just want to go home. Maybe we just really need some...some time apart."

Brice leaned up against a nearby parking meter as the words hit him like a gut punch. "Time apart? Are you breaking up with me?"

Anna looked at him, a tear slipping down her cheek, and said, "I don't know what I'm doing anymore. There's a cab. I gotta go." And just like that, Anna ran into the street, jumped into the back seat and sped away.

Brice stumbled back to the party with his heart in pieces.

****

Back at the video shop, Brice got back to studying for his English final. He still couldn't believe his mother had actually pulled off the impossible with Ms. DeLucca.

He spied a copy of *Cobra* laying in the putaway bin and felt like a horse kicked him in the balls. Brice would never be able to see that tape again without thinking about the fateful day he first met Anna.

They hadn't had any contact since their blowout and Brice took advantage of the extra free time to try and get on the ball with his studies. He'd lost count of all the times he'd picked up the phone to make things right, each time obeying the little voice in his head that told him to hang up, that everything happens for a reason.

Jordan finished putting away some tapes and gave Brice a look. "What's the deal with you and that book?" He nodded at the book open on the counter.

Brice shook his head and said "The deal with this book is that if I don't pass my English final on Friday, I'm fucked. Not kind of fucked, but really, really fucked. And the key to me not being fucked is in this book. So yeah, that's the deal with this book."

Just then, Ted put in a call to the store and said he needed someone to head downtown to his apartment to pick up some freshly minted bootlegs. Brice volunteered. He could get some uninterrupted Hamlet time in on the train ride there. With book in hand, he got going.

The Lower East Side was jumping with activity this time of year. Sidewalk vendors sold every considerable used item on ratty blankets neatly laid out on the sidewalk. A New York Dolls vinyl import caught Brice's eye for a mere five bucks. He made mental note to try and get it for three instead on the way back to the store.

Ted's girl Suzette looked like she'd put on some weight as she opened the door and let Brice in. He marveled at the set up and gave an approving nod.

Ten VCRs going non-stop pumped out near perfect fakes of all the latest releases. The chemical odor of the laser printer that churned out the glossy label replicas for the pirated items reminded Brice of the Mimeograph test papers from grade school. Ted was packing a duffle bag full of tapes when Brice noticed all sorts of baby related items strewn about the apartment.

"Are you guys getting ready to throw a baby shower for someone?"

Ted laughed, pointed to Suzette and said, "Yeah, us. It looks like we've got a bundle of joy showing up in a few months. I hope you're good with kids, because you might have to do a little babysitting on the side."

Brice burst out laughing. "I know how to pop in a 'Thomas the Tank Engine' video and press play."

Ted handed him the duffle bag and said, "Perfect, You're hired!"

Brice shouldered the heavy sack. "Alright, lemme get back uptown or Jordan's gonna have a shit fit if the place gets too busy. Congrats, guys. I'm so happy for you both."

With only three days left until his dreaded English final, Brice mentally prepared himself for the event. Over the past few weeks, he'd spent his time wisely studying his ass off with only a few trips to the Record Emporium to blow off steam and one last powwow with Max and Evan at the mesh cloud. Meanwhile, Granny was lighting candles at church every day.

CHAPTER 21

The clock on the wall read a quarter to ten as Brice paced his bedroom that night, feverishly trying to commit endless scenes of *Hamlet* to memory for his English final in the morning. He planned to hit the hay at ten sharp to be bright-eyed and bushy-tailed for the exam at nine the next morning.

The phone rang as he got ready for bed. It was Anna. And he could barely make out a word she was saying, crying and slurring something about taking too many.

Brice swallowed. "You took too many *what*?" A pause. "Hello?"

The line disconnected.

Heart racing, Brice tried calling back but got a busy signal each time. Speechless, he hung up the phone and sank onto the edge of his bed.

He cut his eyes at the clock – already ten. He stared at his English textbook on the bed next to him. He had a big decision to make.

Within minutes, Brice was dressed and running down the street to catch a cab into the city.

The ride took forty minutes but felt like forty years. The cabbie must have heard the urgency in his voice when he gave the address, because the guy drove like an Indy 500 driver on a quest for a million-dollar purse.

Brice jumped out of the car as they rolled up to the townhouse. He began pounding on the door the instant his feet landed on the doorstep.

It took an entire five minutes for Anna to answer.

He breathed a heavy sigh of relief. She was in rough shape, but she was alive and relatively coherent. He helped her downstairs to the couch. Mel and Raye had apparently been in The Hamptons for a few days and Isis was home sick. Anna began apologizing for everything that had happened and for dragging him into an unwinnable situation, bawling into his chest. "I don't want you to be mad at me. I'm sorry about the party. I don't know what came over me. You and Lindsey have this 'thing'. I know you're just friends and all, but I just felt so jealous and ugly because she's so pretty and I love you so much."

Brice did his best to console her, subtly checking the clock. It was a quarter after eleven now. He could have Anna completely calmed down and into bed by midnight at the latest, which would give him an hour to get back to Brooklyn and get at least six hours of sleep.

Anna got up and said she needed to go to the bathroom. Brice offered to help her get there, but it looked like she could manage on her own. She went inside and closed the door.

But she was gone too long and Brice sensed something was wrong. He jumped up and called her name. She didn't reply. He started banging on the door when he heard the sound of glass crashing on the floor. He tried the knob again. It was locked tight.

He started screaming her name. With no options left, he backed up and started running at full speed, kicking with all his might. The door came loose from the frame and hinges.

Anna lay on the floor in a pool of blood. Empty bottles of prescription drugs and shards of broken glass from the medicine cabinet lay all around her, like some sort of macabre photo shoot. Heedless of the blood and glass, Brice picked her up in his arms and laid her down carefully on the living room floor. He frantically called 911 for an ambulance and did his best to try and make her throw up everything she'd swallowed.

The ambulance arrived in ten minutes. It took another eight to get her to Lenox Hill Hospital. The ER doctors did their best to pump Anna's stomach and keep her breathing. It was touch and go as her heart rate dipped down into dangerous territory more than once.

The beeping sound of a heart monitor woke Brice up from a deep slumber. Anna lay in her hospital bed with tubes and wires sticking out from under her blankets as the overcast morning bled into the room through worn nylon window curtains. She was awake.

Brice looked her over. His voice was so hoarse, he didn't recognize it. "We almost lost you last night."

Anna looked away. "I don't want you to see me like this."

"What the hell were you thinking?" Brice reached for Anna's hand but she moved it away from him. Brice sighed, and it sounded far too weary for someone his age. "There are so many people that love you. *I* love you."

Anna's emerald eyes, once so lively and bright, dimmed with tears that overflowed and streamed down her face. "I'm unlovable Brice, and you're just a kid. It's not right that I've dragged you down into this hole with me. You lied about your age and I lied about everything else. I guess that makes us even."

"But we can work through this together." Desperation had Brice kneeling at the side of her hospital bed, willing to beg for a chance.

Anna's eyes closed. "No, we can't. I have to do this alone. I'm tired of waking up every day not knowing which Anna the world gets to deal with."

Brice's lip trembled. Anna just refused to let him be the hero, just once. "So what do we do?"

With a trembling sigh, Anna said, "I can't answer that right now. I just know I can't keep pretending everything's okay with me." At that moment, Mel, Raye, and Isis burst into the room. They circled around Anna's bed, displacing Brice and unintentionally pushing him back toward the window. Isis looked back at Brice with gratitude shining from her eyes, as if to thank him for saving Anna's life.

He took this as his cue to head back to Brooklyn and slipped out of the room without a sound.

****

By the time Brice worked up the nerve to knock on the door, he found Ms. DeLucca sitting in an empty classroom grading final exams.

She looked up at him, then at the clock on the wall far above his head. "Mr. Laine. Apparently, you're running a little late today. I guess Hamlet will spend his days in eternity wondering why you'd forsaken him. And you'll have to spend the next fall semester in my class, trying to make it up to him."

She went back to grading papers, dismissing him.

But Brice wasn't giving up that easily. He had nothing more to lose.

He approached the teacher's desk and waited for her to look up at him over the rim of her glasses. When she did, he said "I know I messed up. But if I could just explain – "

"Brice," she said, interrupting him, "I know you're gonna find this hard to believe, but I actually do like you. I spoke with your mother. She told me the whole story. How you grew up without a dad, bounced around between relatives, held down a job in the city. I get it. That's why I gave you one final chance to make this right."

Brice slid into in an empty desk. "See, that's the thing. I studied my ass off. I know this stuff like the back of my hand. Last night, I just...I was put in a very bad situation where I had to make a choice: help someone who was in serious trouble or bail on them and make it here back in time."

Ms. DeLucca stopped grading papers, pen poised in the air as she studied Brice. "So you went ahead and helped this person? Knowing full well it would ruin any chance you had at graduating?" She pursed her lips, considering. "Sounds like someone very special."

A sad smile tugged at Brice's mouth. "She's the Ophelia to my Hamlet. Well, maybe a bit more like Juliet, but yeah...I mean..."

Ms. DeLucca grinned and shook her head at the Hamlet reference and said, "Okay. You know what, Brice? You actually caught me in a good mood. So, against my better judgment, I'm going to take you at your word. Everyone that's managed to pass this exam has taken an average of 45 minutes to complete it. You've got 20. I guess we'll just let Ophelia decide your fate."

Standing, she reached over her desk and handed Brice the exam and a pencil. With a look of utter disbelief, Brice grabbed the paper and starting writing.

****

A wide swath of satin caps and gowns shimmered in the midday sun. The soon-to-be graduates broiling on white folding chairs took up half of Fort Brambleton's football field.

The top school administrators slowly read off the names of the graduating class of 1987 in alphabetical order. As a young blonde Christine Kowalski headed towards the stage to receive her diploma, the name Allen Lewis came bellowing out of Principal Feld's bullhorn before his assistant Edna rushed over and pointed to the handwritten name on his clip board that had been added at the last minute.

"Sorry – hold on, Allen," he muttered before belting out a bright

170

and clear *"Brice Laine.* Is Brice here? Great, come on up."

Brice felt like he was flying as he sped towards the stage to accept his hard-fought certificate of validation. Lindsey, Mom, Jordan, Gil, Aunt Maggie and Uncle Amir, Granny, Ted and Suzette all screamed and cheered him on from the sidelines.

Fingers crossed behind his back, Brice wouldn't release them until he was certain that rolled piece of heavy stock paper lay squarely in his hands. He let out a deep sigh of relief as Principal Feld patted him on the back and said, "Good job!" The weight of the world literally lifted from Brice's shoulders. He slapped hands with Max and Evan on the way back to his chair.

As he sat there listening to the dozens of other names being read off the clipboard, he couldn't help but reflect on what a crazy year it had been. The fact that he was actually sitting in a cap and gown holding his high school diploma was literally a miracle. He stared down at the tightly rolled up document. Curiously, it looked like a baton that had been handed off to him for the second leg of some kind of race. Come what may, he'd take it all in stride.

Hundreds of caps shot high into the sky to deafening cheers as the official ceremony came to an end. Brice headed over to his group for some hugging and glad-handing. Max jumped him from behind and shouted directly into his ear, making Brice wince. "We did it, man! I don't know how, but we did it!"

Evan grabbed his buddies around the neck and said, "It's a fucking miracle. The mesh cloud gods musta taken pity on us!"

"Either that or they're sick of us and hope we just move on," Brice said, laughing harder than he could remember doing in a long time. It felt like complete freedom.

Lindsey rushed over, gave each of the boys a big hug and kiss and said, "I am so proud of you guys! This is gonna be such a great Summer!"

Evan unzipped his gown and let out a hearty, "Oh, yeah!"

The joyous event started winding down to its inevitable conclusion. Brice stood shooting the shit with Jordan and Gil when a yellow taxi appeared out of nowhere. It double parked on the street next to the field and stood idling as its female passenger got out and walked towards the group.

Brice turned to take a quick look and started shaking when he realized it was Anna. Even after their breakup, his heart still soared at the sight of her. But how was she here at all?

He turned to Jordan, who made a face and gave an unapologetic shrug. "What? She asked, so I had to tell her."

Brice's knees wobbled as he walked across the field to meet her halfway. Anna wore her trademark summer dress and cowboy boots, her hair two shades lighter, shimmering in the sun.

She cracked a smile that almost brought a tear to his eye; seemed like such a long time since he'd seen it.

"I hope you're not mad," she said, her smoky voice just the way Brice remembered. "I made Jordan tell me."

"No. How could I be mad?"

There was no sound between them for a moment except for the wind rustling through the trees nearby. Anna teared up as she said, "I just wanted to see you one last time before I go."

Brice cocked his head. "Before you go where?"

Anna crossed her arms, staring at the ground as she kicked at a patch of grass. "California. My mother's friend runs a treatment facility out there."

Brice swallowed hard again and again to keep his own hot tears in check. "California? For how long?"

"For as long as it takes for me to get better."

Considering how long she'd been dealing with her issues, that meant...Brice, now with tears streaming down his face asked, "Why so far away? I mean, don't they have places like that here in New York?"

"Brice, you know if I stayed here and we got back together, it would just be a repeat performance of the past. I don't want to put you through all that again. You've got a lot of decisions to make about your future, and I guess I do, too. I think we both just need some time to kind of figure things out. I still love you and I'm sure no matter what happens, I always will. Who knows? Maybe one day our paths will cross again under different circumstances. I can't be of any use to you or anyone else if I'm no use to myself."

Brice was speechless. Each word felt like a stab to the heart. He'd been lying to himself thinking that he'd been getting over her. It took everything in his power to not sob uncontrollably.

Anna tried to lighten the mood. She held his hand, looked over to his group and said, "So, you really brought out the cheering squad for this one, huh?"

Brice wiped his tears away, tried to fake a smile. "I think they're just as shocked as I am that they get to be here for this. The odds were definitely not stacked in my favor." Anna glanced back at the cab, then turned to Brice and said, "Okay. Well, I have to go. The cab's waiting and I've got a plane to catch. I really hate goodbyes. Do you think we can we just hug instead?"

Brice and Anna embraced, his throat closing when he realized the feel of her in his arms at that moment might have to last him forever. She was the first to let go. He stood and watched her walk off, heart in his stomach, the joy of his unexpected graduation all but gone. Anna turned around once and waved as she got into the cab and drove away. Brice walked to the group, catching one last fading glimpse of yellow as Anna's cab sped off towards the airport.

Later that evening, as he sat out on the fire escape smoking the day's last cigarette, Brice thanked God for giving him a pass and helping him make it across the finish line. He blew one final smoke ring into the air and climbed back through the window. He sat in bed playing guitar and thought about Anna's parting words. She was right. He did have a lot of decisions to make about his future. Hopefully, she'd get the help she needed.

Brice relaxed into his mattress, warm thoughts of one last great summer filled with good friends, rock and roll, and plenty of mischief lulling him to sleep. The real world could wait a few more months. You only got to be young once.

EPILOGUE

After a solid week of clean up, roof repairs and trips to the closest home improvement store, things slowly got back to normal in the Laine household.

Hurricane Hilda wound up causing over 19 billion dollars worth of damage to over nine million Florida homeowners in twelve counties. Max, Evan and Lindsey, now all busy with families of their own, had all checked in to make sure everything was okay. It was funny how time had turned such a crazy, carefree rabble into such responsible, thoughtful adults; the New York television channels had been airing around-the-clock coverage of the carnage going down in the sunshine state.

Brice, with his leg wound healing up nicely, prepared the kids for a Sunday trip to see Aunt Maggie and Uncle Amir that was long overdue. Vera had the vacuum running nonstop, sucking up the tiny pieces of debris on the floors that had made it inside through the air vents of the house. "Make sure you bring enough water and emergency supplies with you just in case," she said to Brice when she paused to take a breather. "I heard not every gas station has power up and running at the pumps."

"I'm pretty sure we got everything thing we need."

The kids were taking turns talking on the phone with Grandma up in Brooklyn. He motioned for them to get ready to go. Caleb handed the phone to Brice as he and Mara grabbed their backpacks. "Yeah, Ma. Okay. I'll talk to you during the week. I love you, too. Bye."

Staying behind to clean up, Vera gave the kids each a hug and said, "Be careful and make sure you call me when you get there."

"Got it," Brice said and he gave her a parting kiss as he and the kids headed towards to car, both giggling and pushing each other all the way. Ah, if only Granny were still alive to enjoy those rascals. She was a ball of energy herself up until the very end. She'd passed quietly in her sleep without any prolonged illnesses weighing her down of forcing her to "be a burden to anyone", as she put it. Brice missed her dearly and spoke of her often to the kids.

There wasn't a cloud in the sky as the family minivan pulled out of the cul de sac and onto the main road. Brice popped his cherished Seducer's Charm disc into the CD player and hummed along with every word. The band had slugged it out in the clubs up until the early nineties and had built up one of the biggest unsigned act followings in the tri-state area when they finally inked a deal with a major label. But grunge caught on like a wild fire and within a few months of their debut release had dealt a merciless death blow to every hard rock act in the country, leaving Grant and the rest of Seducer's Charm high and dry. With little or no options left to make a living, Grant had had to act fast, and within six months he had his CDL Class A license and was driving big rigs for the trucking company owned by Tristan's stepdad. After a few years, he and Tristan pooled their resources and started their own company.

Jordan was married with two kids and still living in Brooklyn. He took over the upstairs portion of the house when Gil and his wife retired. Ted and Suzette and their two boys left the city when Video Star eventually folded and headed out to Northern California, where Ted took an executive position at a startup tech firm. Even good old Bob Rock turned his back on his life of debauchery, becoming a born-again Christian after a coke-induced heart attack brought him inches away from the big sleep.

Brice could not believe the devastation still evident all along Interstate 95. Huge metal air conditioning units hung off the ledges of commercial building as if swept aside by giants. Mighty trees that once shaded shopping centers lay there pulled up by the roots and mortally wounded as the constant buzz of chainsaws hummed in the distance. All things considered, Brice and his family had truly dodged a bullet. He checked his fuel gauge before glancing in the rear view to see if his little monsters were catching a cat nap while buckled in the safety of their booster seats.

The Seaview Commons Retirement Community was everything you'd imagine it to be, with well-groomed elderly couples clad in freshly ironed sports apparel zooming along its manicured fairway in shiny white golf carts. Brice glided his vehicle into a free "Guests Only" parking spot and breathed in the fresh ocean air. Maintenance personnel worked at a frenetic pace painting, repairing and reassembling the badly damaged clubhouse. After waking the kids, the trio walked up the cobble stone path straight to unit 641.

Aunt Maggie opened the door with a huge smile. "Well, look who finally showed up for a visit! C'mon in gang. "Amir!" She called her husband over her shoulder. "Brice and the kids are here! Where are my kisses?" Aunt Maggie bent down to dole out some smooches as Uncle Amir joined in on the love fest. After a kiss for his aunt and uncle, Brice headed into the kitchen for some much-needed coffee.

Uncle Amir built pillow forts with the kids while Brice and Aunt Maggie set up in the living room to chat. Just outside the window, gleaming pleasure vessels with scantily clad foreign girls lazily glided up and down the Intracoastal. One would have never known such a tempest of a storm had taken place just a week ago.

Brice looked around the apartment and said, "It's nice to have the power back on, huh? So, I guess everything else is back to normal?"

Aunt Maggie took a sip of coffee, nodding. "Pretty much, though your poor uncle had to wait two hours the other day for gas. The supermarkets are still a zoo, but other than that, we really can't complain."

He couldn't have asked for better news. Everyone he loved was alright. He smiled, patting the back of her free hand. "That's great. Our cable and Internet is still out, so I feel a little cut off from the outside world, but yeah. It could have been a complete disaster, so I guess I'm not gonna complain, either."

The kids ran into the room and started playing on the floor. Brice took a look over at the coffee table and noticed a thick stack of newspapers and said, "I see your beloved Sunday *New York Times* delivery is back on schedule."

"You know I can't live without my Sunday *Times*!" she said, chuckling lightly, then her smile suddenly dimmed. "Oh, before I forget honey, I just wanted to let you know how sorry I am to hear about your friend."

Brice frowned. "Sorry about my friend? What are you talking about?"

She picked up the "Obituary" section of the paper to show him and said, "Oh, I figured you must have heard about your friend Anna from back in New York. She passed away a few days ago. I just read her obit this morning."

Anna. To his utter amazement, Brice's hand shook a little when he reached for the page. He could only scan the small paragraph as scenes from his youth and the time they'd spent together burst like fireworks through his mind.

A deep, profound sadness welled up in him. Brice's voice quivered as he sat up and said, "Uh, no. I...I hadn't heard. We lost touch years ago."

Aunt Maggie frowned and clicked her tongue. "What a shame, such a young girl...to die so soon." She opened up the paper and started to read: "Miller, Anna, beloved daughter of noted Broadway playwright, composer, and author Garland Miller and singer Raye Miller, died in New York City late Wednesday evening from injuries sustained in an automobile accident on the West Side Highway. She was forty-three years old. Ms. Miller, a graduate of Marymount Manhattan College and Columbia Clinical University, was a licensed behavioral therapist and used her talent and training in assisting developmentally disabled children at the Harlem Center for Special Achievers. She is preceded in death by her father Garland Miller in 1968 and is survived her mother, noted actress and singer Raye Miller and Stepfather Mel Willis. A nondenominational memorial service will be held this Saturday at the Wallace J. Turner Funeral Chapel. In lieu of flowers, donations can be made to the American Humane Society."

When his aunt reached for his hand, Brice took it. He sipped down the last of his coffee with unshed tears standing in his eyes and said a prayer for sweet Anna.

It was a solemn ride back home. Luckily, both kids stayed asleep as the slow aching throb of mourning crept into Brice's soul. Unable to help himself, he kept running through all the scenes – the good, the bad and the ugly. He had no regrets about how his life turned out. He had a beautiful, caring wife, two great kids and a good, steady job. Still, he felt a strange sense of longing for the one last goodbye that would never come.

There was no rhyme or reason as to why some people get to stay and some must leave. If everything Catholic school pounded into his head about heaven was true, maybe someday they'd both meet again.

The End

Made in the USA
Middletown, DE
08 May 2024